TEE-BO
The Great Hort Hunt

BEHIND THE WATERFALL CURTAIN

"There's a cave back in there; I'm sure of it," Cam said. "It could be the way to the country of the Horts."

There was a dark hole in the rocks behind the falls, large enough to step into, if one bent over, and lined with thick moss, over which water trickled and streamed in rivulets.

Carlyle shivered. "Can you still hear the Horts?" she whispered. For answer, her brother handed her the stone. Her eyes widened as she listened. "It's much louder, but it's so sad. I wonder what dreadful thing could have happened to them."

"Hah!" snorted Tee-Bo. "We'd better wonder what dreadful thing might happen to us!"

"I'm going to see where this cave leads," Cam said firmly. "You can stay here, if you like."

"I'm going, too," Carlyle said quickly, "so don't go too fast!"

Tee-Bo rolled his eyes and shook his head, muttering, "Forevermore!" as he bounded after them.

TEE-BO

THE INCREDIBLE TALKING DOG

leads the way, in

THE GREAT HORT HUNT

by Mary Burg Whitcomb

illustrated by David K. Stone

cover by Olindo Giacomini

GOLDEN PRESS

Western Publishing Company, Inc.
Racine, Wisconsin

CONTENTS

1

Mrs. Firstpenny's Problem

Summer was advancing into fall, and vacation days were almost at an end. Father was beginning to be fidgety about his new schedule at the university, where he was a professor of history. Mother was spending much time at the sewing machine, making school clothes, and even more time sketching the autumn foliage in Riverview, where they lived—at 37 Selah Road, to be exact.

Cameron was hanging by his knees from a tree limb in the front yard, and Carlyle was curled up in the nearby hammock, a book on her lap.

"Have you really read twenty-seven books this

11

summer?" the boy asked his sister.

"Twenty-seven?" She wrinkled her nose. "I guess so."

"Mother told Mrs. Flanella that."

"Twenty-seven I hadn't read before. That's not counting about ten others I read over."

"You read awfully fast."

"I know." Carly stretched, her eyes straying back to the page she held with her thumb. "Sometimes I wish I didn't."

Swinging slowly back and forth, Cam was picking pebbles from the ground and trying to see how many he could toss into the watering can while he was upside down. He was, if anything, more fidgety than Father; he wished his sister would stop reading and go skating with him.

"One more week until school starts," he sighed. *Plunk!* He dropped a pebble neatly into the can.

His sister moaned, rolled her eyes, showed her teeth savagely, and groaned, "Ugh, I know." Then she smiled. "It'll be fun. I can't wait."

"There's still time for one adventure"—Cam brightened—"one more adventure before school starts!"

"Father says we ought to eliminate adventures. We have too many," Carlyle murmured, reading while she talked.

"That's mostly because of Tee-Bo," Cam retorted. He whistled, then called, "Tee-Bo! Here, boy! Where is he?"

"Right there, under the porch—asleep. He said to call him if we go somewhere."

Of course, no one but the children could hear the dog talk. Ever since they had eaten the berries from the thimbleberry bush, back at Monte Rio, on a vacation, they had been able to hear Tee-Bo talk, as plain as day. Carlyle had even brought two of the dust-covered berries home with her, just in case they should lose this strange ability. She kept them hidden in a silver stamp box in her dresser drawer.

Mother came out onto the porch, two threaded needles pinned to her blouse and a puff of flour on her chin.

"Children," she called, "I would like you to take this Tenderberry Pie to Mrs. Firstpenny and ask her for her hundred-year-old recipe for gingerbread. She said she would be home all day."

Idora Firstpenny lived on the other side of the woods, past Farrow's Pond. Her name had been Idora Leora Feora, but when she married Mr. Firstpenny, forty-seven years ago, she discarded the middle part. "It was too pretentious," she told everyone.

The road was the quickest route to her house, but it was more fun to take the path that led through the woods. Mother hadn't said *hurry;* she had just said *go.* Tee-Bo went with them, of course. In the forest, he had many friends that he liked to keep in touch with—and a few in the pond.

Yesterday there had been a wind, and now the forest floor was carpeted with yellow leaves. Cam leaped and ran and finally threw himself on the ground. "I wish I could sleep in the woods all night," he said, staring through the branches at the sky.

"Hah!" scoffed Tee-Bo, who was panting and waiting for them to go on. "One loud croak out of my old friend Matchlock, and you'd scurry home faster than I could."

"Who's Matchlock?" asked Carlyle, shifting the Tenderberry Pie to her other hand.

"The wartiest old toad in Farrow's Pond," Tee-Bo answered. "Knows all, sees all. He's made up all the rules for generations of toads in these parts, and he thinks he's handsome."

"Do you *talk* to him?" Carlyle wondered what she would say if she could talk to a toad. (Talking to a dog seemed perfectly natural by now.)

"When I see him, which isn't often. Once he was caught in a hollow log by a flash flood, and he lived there for a hundred years, until another flood let him out—and *that* was nearly a hundred years ago, so I know he's pretty old."

"Do you believe him?" Cam asked. "Look what I found—a piece of agate." He held out his hand for them to see.

"Oh, I've heard that they do live to be pretty old." Tee-Bo turned his head and sniffed the boy's hand. "What's that?"

"Just a piece of agate, I guess." It was a bluish green stone, about the size of a quarter, with one rough edge, as if it had been broken from a larger piece.

"Can't we go?" asked Carlyle, wishing she had found the fragment, it was so unusual. "I'm tired of carrying this old pie."

Cam was standing on tiptoe, stretching his neck out as far as it would go.

"*Brek-ek-ek-ek, ko-ax, ko-ax, ko-ax,*" he was saying, his mouth opening and shutting and his eyes blinking just as a toad's do.

"Great day in the morning!" cried Tee-Bo, jumping with fright. "You sound exactly like my friend Matchlock!"

"Oh"—Carlyle stamped her foot, with a great sigh —"that's just something Father says when I ask him if I can read one more chapter. Come on!" She looked at her brother curiously. "You do it much better than Father."

"I *did* sound like an old toad, now, didn't I?" Cam

asked, skipping and running ahead, the dog at his heels.

"As like as two peas," Tee-Bo agreed. "Gave me a start."

"I've never been able to do that before," the boy said, and for the rest of the way, he wore a thoughtful expression.

When they reached Mrs. Firstpenny's, Idora was on her knees in a back bedroom, going through the contents of a small trunk.

"I'm looking for a good-luck charm," she explained, after calling to them to come in, "an amulet given to Grandfather Percy by a Sioux chieftain he had befriended."

"An omelette that old," remarked Tee-Bo, "would hardly be worth keeping, I'd say." Mrs. Firstpenny, of course, could not understand Tee-Bo's words.

"Amulet," Carlyle said, with a look.

"Yes, my dear," Idora continued, "a good-luck amulet that, many years ago, belonged to a Sioux chieftain. I can't seem to find it anywhere."

"It can't be a very good charm," Tee-Bo declared, returning Carlyle's look. "There aren't many Sioux chieftains left."

Idora shut the trunk and pushed it back under the bed. "The oddest things have been happening," she told the children, taking them to the kitchen for cookies and milk. "First off, someone—or something —took all the eggs out of the hen house and then stole the chickens, every last one of them."

"Can't you find them anywhere?" asked Carlyle.

"And then," replied Idora, who had a peculiar way of never answering a question directly, "the very next day, they all came marching back home!"

"Even the eggs?" Tee-Bo asked, astonished.

"That's why I wanted the good-luck charm," Idora went on. "Strange things have been happening for the past month, I do declare."

"Like what?" asked the children, feeling sorry for her.

"Living at the edge of the woods, you see, my dears," Idora continued, "a body can expect the wild folk to call now and then, and it would be mighty lonely without them." She thumbed her apron absently as she spoke. "We have an understanding of sorts, and they are all polite and friendly, so none of them has ever unlocked my hen house before, or let poor Heavingham out of the barn"—Heavingham was the horse—"and frightened the wits out of him, or tied all the arms and legs of my wash together on the clothesline, or put the milk pail upside down over my chimney. What a sorry mess I had to tidy up then! It took me two days, I declare!"

"Mrs. Firstpenny," said Cam, swallowing the last

moist cookie crumb, "would you like us to help you find out who is doing this?"

"For a month," Idora said, sighing heavily as she picked up the dishes, "I haven't known what to expect next. Here's the gingerbread recipe your mother asked for, the dear soul. I haven't had a Tenderberry Pie in years. You must thank her for me. And your papa, dear man that he is, is he still working hard on his . . . uh . . . Spanish dictionary?"

"Mongolian," said Carlyle.

"Another one? Well, I declare. Please give him my regards."

"We will." Carlyle nodded. "Would you like us—"

"Now, don't linger too long in the woods," advised the old lady kindly, patting their heads. "You can ride Heavingham on your next visit. He threw a shoe when he was frightened, and he's down the road a piece, at the blacksmith's. If you see anyone near the hen house, let me know!"

Cam put the recipe in his shirt pocket, and they started for home, waving to Idora standing in her doorway.

"I guess she doesn't want anyone to help her find out who's been doing all those things," Cam said.

"Whoever it is, they're just plain mean," Carlyle declared, frowning. "If Mr. Firstpenny was still living, he'd fix them. Did you see anyone by the hen house or around the barn, Tee-Bo?"

"Only chickens," he answered. "I checked the place out and couldn't find anything unusual. I'll talk to Heavingham when he gets back, but he's worse than Mrs. Firstpenny about answering questions."

They had entered the woods now, where it was cool and still. Farrow's Pond lay ahead, and the fragrance of water and willows drifted to them on the breeze. Cam, who had been silent for some time, suddenly stopped, looking back over his shoulder with a startled expression.

"Did you see that?" he exclaimed.

"That flicker?" asked Carlyle. "I see the one up in that tree."

"Not the flicker." Cam spoke in a whisper. "I thought I saw someone behind us."

They waited for a moment, listening, but the forest was suddenly still. Even the flicker, its great eyes fixed on them from behind the foliage, did not stir.

"I'll fall back," Tee-Bo muttered, "and take a look."

"Don't!" whispered Cam nervously. "Just stay close. I *know* I saw someone, but he's gone."

"What did he look like?" his sister asked as they went on. "Was it a man or what?"

"I couldn't tell. I just caught a glimpse of someone behind a tree."

"How could you see him if he was *behind* a tree?" Tee-Bo asked.

"Because he looked around the tree at us, that's how," Cam answered, rather crossly.

He walked on, taking the small stone from his pocket and tossing it into the air from time to time. Then he began to whistle, but instead of his regular whistle (which was really less than outstanding), a beautiful birdcall poured forth—a warbling, clear and strange, that echoed sweetly through the woods.

"Oh, Cam!" his sister cried, stopping to listen. "How did you do that?"

Cam, with a look of astonishment, was standing perfectly still. "I . . . I don't know," he answered and very cautiously pursed his lips to try it again. This time another, even more beautiful, birdcall filled the air.

"Forevermore," Tee-Bo said, staring at the boy in wonder, "where did you learn that?"

Cam was looking very embarrassed now. "I . . . I don't think I did it," he replied slowly.

"You certainly did," his sister replied. "I was looking right at you."

"It was something inside me," Cam said. "That's what did it."

"Then you swallowed a live bird," Tee-Bo retorted, "and you ought to have told us!"

Cam didn't answer. He walked on hurriedly, holding his head down, as though something bothered him. He refused to talk. Nor would he whistle again, although his sister begged him to.

2

A Face in the Woods

When they had walked for some time in silence, Carlyle stopped and looked wistfully in the direction of the falls, which could not even be heard at this distance.

"I wonder if the falls are full," she sighed, half to herself.

"We can go and look, if you like," Cam offered, feeling a little ashamed of himself and knowing she wouldn't ask because he was in such a cross mood.

So they took the long way around the pond, going over the path that led to the falls. This was really the prettiest part of Love Creek, this quarter of a mile through the woods before the stream entered Farrow's Pond. Trees bordered it thickly on both sides, screening the sunlight so that the water appeared deep and black, and the banks were lined with ferns of all kinds, tall ones, higher than Cam's head, and small, delicate ones that seemed to tremble ever so slightly. Children of many generations had worn a footpath along the gentle stream, but now this, too, was almost overgrown, because no one came here anymore. Around a bend farther up, the trees parted, and the creek widened—in fact, doubled in size— forming into the falls, a musical miniature waterfall, dropping over a wall of rock five or six feet high, spilling in a glassy sheet and frothing prettily as the cascade met the water below. It was not dark here. Sunbeams danced on the surface of the water, while silvery droplets and rainbow sprays skipped up and down and across the ribbon of water as it fell.

Tee-Bo had scampered ahead and now waited for them, lapping the sweet, cold water.

"We ought to have a picnic here," Carlyle said, throwing herself down full length at the edge of the stream and drinking deeply. Cam was about to do the same, when suddenly he stopped, with the same startled expression that had appeared earlier on his face.

"What's that?"

"What's what?" Carlyle asked, holding her hair back out of the water.

Tee-Bo ran up to them, water running off his chin whiskers. "Don't tell me it's him again!" he growled.

"Listen!" Cam whispered. "Just *listen!*"

He was staring across the water at the falls, as if there were some strange apparition there, in full view, that the others could not see. They listened intently for a moment, and then Cam exclaimed, "There! Did you hear that?"

"I didn't hear anything but the falls," Carlyle whispered. "Is that what you mean?"

"Of course not," he replied. "Didn't you hear someone singing?"

"I certainly didn't," Tee-Bo said, "and I'm getting nervous—which means we'd better leave, pronto."

"Wait a minute," Cam whispered. "Don't say anything for a minute."

He stood there, listening and frowning, then looked from his sister to Tee-Bo. "You honestly didn't hear anyone singing?"

They both answered no, Tee-Bo adding soberly, "I guess your ears are even better than mine."

"Let's go," Cam said suddenly. He was cross again and began walking very fast along the path toward home.

"Who would be singing way out here?" Carlyle

whispered as she and the dog hurried after him.

"The funny part of it," Tee-Bo panted, "is that Cam hears it and we don't, but if we say anything, he'll just get angry again."

"I know," the little girl agreed, and for the rest of the way home, she sang (but under her breath so no one would hear):

> "Crosspatch, draw the latch,
> Sit by the fire and spin;
> Take a cup and drink it up,
> Then call your neighbors in."

At dinner that evening, Father was discoursing, as usual, on his favorite topic: the great Mongolian race and the glories of its past. He was helping his friend and colleague, Dr. Arthur Wee-Hee, to compile the first English-Mongolian dictionary, which, they estimated, would take them about nine years to complete.

"My dear," Father was saying, having finished a second helping of Posh-Tosh and Rhubarb Pie (an original recipe of Mother's), "it was the great Genghis Khan himself who exempted from taxes the ministers of all religions, the poor, doctors, and other wise men—"

"The *poor doctors?*" Mother inquired, somewhat absently, for she was mentally concocting a new pie recipe to be called Khan Pecan Chiffon.

"The poor *and* the doctors," Father corrected.

"The poor couldn't pay taxes, anyway, could they?" asked Tee-Bo, who, from his rug in the corner, was listening to every word.

"Tee-Bo," Carlyle said, "don't interrupt."

"Interrupt? Hah!" The dog showed all his teeth in a grin. "Neither time nor tide can interrupt Father on *that* subject. I'll wager every member of this family, including yours truly, knows more Mongolian history than any six Mongolians put together!"

"We know more than Genghis Khan, anyway," Cam offered. "He certainly couldn't have known what happened after he died."

"My point, exactly," agreed Tee-Bo, snapping his teeth together in satisfaction.

Father was favoring Cameron with a long look. "I'm sure that dog is profoundly interested in our conversation," he remarked, somewhat enviously, because the children and Tee-Bo always seemed to understand one another completely.

"He likes to listen," Cam said, with a grin.

"Perhaps," Father went on, somewhat grandly, "you had better explain to him that it is not the history of the *mongrels* we are discussing. He may be a bit confused on that point."

"Oh, *Father*," Carlyle said, while Mother just raised her eyebrows. But Cam made the mistake of snickering, though he tried to hide it.

"Laugh if you wish, boy," Tee-Bo said, looking injured as he got to his feet, "but if *my* father had ever made a remark like that, I'd have been greatly disappointed in him. Of course," he went on rather bitterly, "everyone knows that the worst puns ever made are conceived in the minds of history professors."

Mother was rising from the table, with a look of concern. "I brought a bone home from the market," she told Tee-Bo, "but I forgot to give it to you." Opening the refrigerator, she removed the bone and held it out to him. "You've hurt his feelings," she said to Father. "He's really very sensitive."

Tee-Bo rolled his eyes at this. "Angel!" he said and *(snap!)* fastened his teeth onto the bone. "Remember," he said grimly as he left to go out the back door, "a pun is the lowest form of wit."

"I am in the unfortunate position," Father was saying, "of a man, the head of the household, in competition with a dog."

"Dear"—Mother patted his shoulder and looked at him anxiously—"did you want that bone?"

While Mother and Father were exchanging ominous glances, Carlyle spoke up hastily. "Mrs. Firstpenny has been having a lot of trouble," she said. "Cam and I offered to help her, but she didn't pay any attention to us."

"What kind of trouble?" Father asked at once, for, behind his academic posture, he had a soft heart that could not bear to see anyone or anything suffer.

The children told them about the chickens and poor old Heavingham, the horse, and the milk pail put over the chimney, causing the whole inside of the house to be covered with soot.

"I'll look at my schedule," Father said, "and go out to see her sometime tomorrow."

"You have a lecture at one tomorrow," Mother reminded him.

"Well, hang it all," Father replied, standing up and rumpling his hair, "I just may be a little late for it. We certainly can't have old ladies being harassed, without doing something about it."

"I'll go with you," Mother said. "I've been wanting to do a sketch of her old barn."

The next day, they got into Old Bessie and drove off to see Mrs. Firstpenny, returning shortly before lunch. During the night, someone had painted, in large, slipshod letters across her front porch beams, the words HEN HOUSE, and Father was furious. Mrs. Firstpenny had refused to let anyone tell the sheriff, saying these were pranks that would probably stop before long. Father had gone back to town, had bought white paint, and had applied two generous coats over the offending letters.

"I'll come back Sunday," he told Mrs. Firstpenny, "and put on a third coat."

Now he had to eat lunch in a hurry and drive off to give his lecture, a white paint smudge on one ear, another on his nose, and several in his hair.

"Let's be glad it isn't a beauty contest," he said as he was leaving.

"If it were, you'd win, paint or no paint," Mother said firmly, kissing him good-bye.

The children were out in the front garden, Carlyle in the hammock and Cam just sitting on the front steps. He was still in a cross mood, and Tee-Bo, lying nearby, regarded him dolefully.

"I don't know why *you're* in a bad mood," Tee-Bo remarked. "Father wasn't making fun of *you*. Puns!" He ended with a sniff of disdain.

"Father was only joking," Carlyle said, patting him. "I wish *you'd* stop being cross, too," she sighed, looking at her brother.

"You'd be, too, if you were me," Cam answered. "You and Tee-Bo think I was just making that up about the voice I heard—and probably about the face I saw, too. But I wasn't."

"Why don't we go back there and look?" Carlyle said, rolling out of the hammock. "This time Tee-Bo and I might hear it."

"I'm against it!" the dog answered promptly. "It's nice and safe right here."

"What if we do hear it?" Cam asked. "What then?"

"At least, you'll stop being cross."

They ran in to get permission and two apples, Tee-Bo nervously trotting at their heels. "But remember," he warned them, when they were on their way a moment later, "curiosity killed the cat."

"The cat's not going," Cam said.

"Anyway," added Carlyle, "satisfaction brought him back."

They hurried along the river's edge to the bridge and were soon on the path to Farrow's Pond.

"It seems quieter than yesterday," Carlyle whispered, trying to look around in all directions at once.

"It's because you're listening harder," Tee-Bo whispered back.

They were within hearing distance of the falls, when Carlyle said, quite calmly and without altering her pace, "Cam, I see him. He's right behind us."

Cam stopped so suddenly that he tripped Tee-Bo.

"Keep on going," hissed Carlyle, "but look back!"

"I don't see anyone," Tee-Bo complained nervously. "Are you sure, Carly?"

"I don't see anyone, either," Cam whispered. "How close is he?"

The three of them were huddled together on the

narrow path, which made walking difficult.

"He's dodging behind the trees so we won't see him," the little girl said, "but I saw him, all right!"

"Forevermore," moaned Tee-Bo, his chin whiskers doing a mad dance. "How can I chase what I can't see?"

By now they had almost reached the falls.

"Where is he now, Carly?" Cam whispered.

"He's gone," she replied, standing still, her gaze searching the wood. "I don't see him at all."

"What did he look like?" her brother asked excitedly. "Did he have a long, sort of thin face?"

She nodded. "A mean face. Pointed and awfully pale."

"I don't see how you could see him when no one else could," Cam fretted.

"That's what happened with you yesterday," the dog reminded him.

"I wonder why he follows us," Carlyle said. "That's what puzzles me."

"Weren't you scared, Carly?" her brother asked.

"A little bit, at first, but then I saw him run from one tree to another, and he isn't any bigger than we are!"

The other two stared at her in surprise. "Really?" asked Cam. "No bigger than us?"

"Is he a little *kid*?" Tee-Bo queried.

"I don't think so," she replied. "He's little and thin, but he looks old—" She broke off suddenly, her eyes widening in surprise. "Ssh!" she warned them. "Now I hear it!"

"Hear what?" cried the dog, coming to life quickly. "Is he back again?"

"No, but I hear it. I hear the singing."

They remained standing near the falls, Tee-Bo and Cam staring at Carlyle, whose eyes were growing wider every moment.

"Oh," she sighed at length, "it's pretty, but it's sad!"

"Where is it coming from?" Tee-Bo asked.

"There's only one place it *could* be coming from," she answered thoughtfully, "and that's behind the falls."

3
The Lapis Lazuli

None of them made any effort to approach the falls. They stood close together in the sunlight, looking at one another and wondering what to do.

"It's such a sad song," Carlyle said finally, "that I think maybe we're intruding."

They began retracing their steps through the wood. Though they carefully watched every tree and shrub, there was no sign of the little man with the long, mean face, and they crossed the bridge toward home without seeing him again.

They had just finished their evening meal, when Carlyle reached into the pocket of her blouse and, with a small exclamation of surprise, took something from it and gave it to her brother. Father, who had been discoursing on the Mongols, regarded her with patient curiosity.

"And what is this?" he asked politely, finding, for the moment, something more interesting than his topic.

"It's Cam's. Mother asked me to give it to him this morning, but I forgot."

"I found it in your shirt pocket," Mother said, "when I washed clothes."

Father held out his hand. "Why, that's very nice. May I see it?"

He held the stone between his fingers and examined it, turning it this way and that.

"Is it agate, Father?" Cam asked, while everyone's eyes were fastened on the broken bit of stone.

"No," Father said slowly, "it is not agate. It's lapis lazuli."

Cam's eyes widened. "Is it valuable?"

"It was to the ancients. It was believed to be their sapphire." Father smiled at him. "As it is, it has no value, Son, but it has been polished and appears to have broken off of something that could have had some value."

"My sister had a lapis lazuli ring," Mother mused. "She used to let me wear it."

When asked where he had found it, Cam said it had been lying in the leaves near Mrs. Firstpenny's house, and this started Mother and Father talking about the old lady, until it was the children's bedtime.

The next morning, Carlyle had to stand and have hems measured for new dresses, and then both children went with Mother to Oliphant's Boot Shop for school shoes. It was one of the hottest days of the year, and Mother was glad to get back home.

"I don't know whether to go under the sprinkler or into the community pool or just lie in a tub of cold water," she sighed, but, of course, she ended up by cleaning both bathrooms and trying out her new recipe for Khan Pecan Chiffon Pie.

The children had been given permission to go as far as Mrs. Firstpenny's and back, but they were not to bother the old lady, who'd had enough troubles lately.

It was cool in the forest, and they stopped at Farrow's Pond to sit on the grass in the shade.

"No one lives near the forest but Mrs. Firstpenny," Carlyle said thoughtfully. "I wish someone lived *in* it—someone who could tell us what's happening."

"That someone would have to be very wise and would have to live right here—" her brother began, then stopped short, his eyes meeting his sister's.

"Matchlock!" cried both children together. "Let's find Matchlock and ask him!"

Tee-Bo looked doubtful. "He sleeps a lot, and he only talks when he feels like it. He's not half as smart as he thinks he is, either."

"He ought to know everything that goes on in the woods, though," Carlyle declared as they went toward Farrow's Pond, "if he's as old as he says he is."

The pond looked quite empty, with the willows trailing their long branches at the edge of the water and the surrounding hillsides reflected in its unmoving surface.

Tee-Bo called Matchlock several times, while the children waited.

"He lives under that old sunken log out there," the dog explained, "but I don't think he'll come up. It's too hot. Why don't you call him, Cam?"

But when Cam tried to say *"Brek-ek-ek-ek, ko-ax, ko-ax,"* which had sounded exactly like a toad before, he simply couldn't do it.

"That's funny. It was easy before. . . ." He whistled and then looked chagrined. "Now I can't even whistle like I did."

They threw pebbles and sticks into the water and tried calling Matchlock all at once, until the woods fairly echoed, but there was no reply. Just as they were leaving, quite disappointed, Carlyle looked back over her shoulder and noticed something peculiar.

"That's a funny-looking rock," she said, pointing at the nearest edge of the pond. "It wasn't there before."

Tee-Bo stared. "Right," he said, nodding. "It isn't a rock, either." He ran back to the water's edge. "All right, Matchlock, how long have you been here?"

The water rippled, and the rock moved. Suddenly the children saw that it was really the head of the biggest toad they had ever seen or heard of.

"Heh-heh-heh"—the old fellow had a voice like iron bellows—"all afternoon, waiting to see who'd discover me first, by thunder! Great disguise, eh?"

He had emerged halfway out of the water and crouched there, a giant of a fellow, blinking rakishly and nodding. A deep, grating chuckle issued from his throat as he surveyed the trio on the bank.

Tee-Bo gave him a look of disgust. "I might have known you'd do something like this."

"You might at least have answered," Carlyle told him. "That was hardly very polite of you, Mr. Matchlock."

"And who are *you?*" The old toad blinked.

Tee-Bo introduced them. "These are my friends Cameron and Carlyle McRae. I've told you about them."

"Throwing sticks and stones," grumbled Matchlock. "A fine way to waken a body from a delicious morsel of sleep."

"We apologize," Cam said, "but we had to ask you something. You're probably the only one who knows."

"Humph!" retorted Matchlock. "Who says I'll tell? I'm no blabbermouth."

Carlyle was staring at him earnestly. "You're certainly the biggest toad I've ever seen. You must be the biggest one in the whole world."

"Heh-heh. In my family, we're all big—big and handsome."

"Handsome is as handsome does," quoted Tee-Bo, with a significant look at Matchlock.

"Well"—Matchlock returned the look—"if you're such an educated fellow, why don't *you* tell them what they want to know?"

"Because I haven't known the forest long enough," replied the dog sensibly. "Ask him, Cam, and he might do us the honor of answering."

"We saw a face in the woods," the boy began promptly, "and someone followed us. We think it was a man, not very big, with a mean face. Then we heard singing—behind the waterfall. My sister and I both heard it."

The old toad remained silent for a moment, staring and blinking. At length he yawned—a tremendous gape—and snapped his jaws together.

"Is that all?" he asked lazily. They nodded, and he went on. "Well, I'd say too many green apples." He began to move, and streams of water coursed down his great back. "You've eaten too many green apples, and you're having nightmares." He began turning slowly, preparing to submerge.

"Don't you know *anything* about it?" Cam asked in astonishment.

"Nope. Not a thing." The water was beginning to bubble around him.

"He does too!" Tee-Bo whispered indignantly. "He just won't tell!"

"Mr. Matchlock," Carly called after him, "come back, or we'll cast a spell over you!"

The old toad paused. "You'll *what?*"

"We'll cast a spell over you," the little girl said firmly, "and all the water in Farrow's Pond will dry up—unless you tell us what you know."

"You can't do it!" said the toad crossly but staying where he was.

"Yes, I can!"

Matchlock looked at her curiously. "Do you really know an incantation—that is, a *spell?* A real one?"

Carly squeezed her eyes shut. "I know a terrible one. It goes like this—"

"Oh, don't d-do it!" Matchlock spluttered. "Don't be so quick, my young friend!"

"It won't work unless I cross my arms and hold on to my ears—like this."

Again he stopped her. "Now, don't be too rash, little girl," he cautioned her. "Couldn't you just *say* the incantation? But don't hold your ears, mind you! Can't I just hear it, without the terrible spell?"

"I suppose so," she replied.

"Then do it!" Matchlock was shivering in fearful delight. "Say the incantation! Say it! Say it!"

"Not unless you promise first to tell us what you know," Cam put in, wondering what in the world his sister was up to.

"All right! All right!" Matchlock answered feverishly. "I'll tell you what you want to know! First the incantation—but not the spell!"

Carlyle hung her arms at her sides and began, in a deep and solemn voice:

> "Inmudeelsare,
> Infurtaris,
> Inoaknoneis—
> Doesyourmareeathay?"

She let her voice trail off into a long, hollow whisper.

Matchlock was shivering so hard that the water was frothing about him.

"Oh, that's lovely! That's horrid! That's positively

hair-raising!" he sputtered. "Say it again! Say it again!"

Cam spoke up quickly. "She mustn't. It's too awful. But if you insist, she might say it *one* more time, after you've kept your promise, that is."

Matchlock gave a great sigh, his shivering fading by degrees. "A bargain's a bargain," he agreed. "Let me just duck under once, to cool off." He submerged and returned to the surface almost at once, regarding them with the most serious expression he had worn yet. "I can only tell you a little, being a fellow of considerable honor, y'know, and—ah—we'd best start with the singing you heard."

"It was very sad," Carly told him.

"That was the voice of the Hort." Matchlock nodded. "I hear it often. Indeed, it's enough to make a body weep."

"Did you say *Hort?*" questioned Tee-Bo. "You've never mentioned that name before."

"What is a Hort?" the children asked.

Matchlock stirred, and the water rippled over his back. "The Horts live in the country behind the waterfall. They were there when my great-great-granddaddy was a tadpole, and as far as anyone knows, they were there when the world began—if not before."

4
The Door in the Rock Grotto

The trio on the bank received this incredible information in complete silence. Observing this, the old toad swelled slightly with importance (not hard for a toad to do) and went on, in a melancholy tone:

"The Horts are probably the finest inhabitants of the whole forest—heh-heh, after us toads, of course—though they believe they live *outside* and we live *inside*. We once visited often, but not anymore. No, not anymore."

"Why not," asked Cam, "if you're friends?"

"They're friends to all," Matchlock replied. "Indeed, it was Courtly Hort himself who helped free me from a log where I had been imprisoned for one hundred years, after a flash flood, although he had to come out to do it—I mean *in*."

"Is there really a country behind the waterfall?" Carlyle asked. "A whole *country?*"

"Certainly," Matchlock retorted. "If there were not, where would the Horts dwell? Look here, I'm drying out. It's much too warm for me. Can't you hurry up? I want to hear that deliciously shivery and horrible incantation again!"

"Why are the Horts sad?" Cam asked.

"You shouldn't have asked that," the old toad replied. "They're my friends, and I oughtn't to blab about them. Couldn't you go ask them yourself? Only watch out for Uncle Rotten Hort. He's tricky, and he's mean; I'll go bail for *that*." Since they all looked astonished at this, Matchlock went on to explain. "His is the face you've been seeing. Probably been spying on you and trying to steal something. He's a great thief and a rogue. Not handsome like us toads, either." Matchlock tried to look over his shoulder, failed, and began to groan. "Really," he begged, "I'm drying up! Please say your dreadful incantation once more, little girl, and let me go!"

"Wait a minute," Cameron interrupted. "How can we get to the country behind the waterfall? Won't we drown?"

"I never thought of that," the old fellow answered slowly, "but, of course, there must be a way. The Horts come out—or they used to, before their great trouble."

"What trouble?" they asked, but Matchlock said he just could not tell them, and the children, seeing that he was drying up fast, felt sorry for him and thanked him for the information.

"And thank *you* for the incantation!" he called back as he dipped lower into the cool water. "One more time, remember!"

So Carlyle repeated the same words, in the deep silence of the forest, and when Matchlock was clear under the water, they could see the shivery bubbles rising to the surface and shuddering as they burst.

They went immediately to the falls but were disappointed again, for there was nothing to be heard now except the gentle murmuring of the water as it spilled over the rocks.

"Well," Cam decided, taking a seat on a flat boulder near the stream, "it's time to take stock of our evidence and come up with a few conclusions."

"You sound like Father," commented Tee-Bo.

"If it please the court," Carlyle put in solemnly, "I'd like to—"

"Father's a history professor," protested the dog, "not a lawyer."

Cam ignored this. "Continue," he said grandly.

"There are a few pieces to this puzzle that don't fit," the little girl finished.

"Such as?" queried her brother, tossing a pebble into the air and catching it, while listening closely.

"For one thing, Your Honor, sometimes we hear the Horts, and sometimes we don't."

Cam nodded. "True."

"And I don't hear them at all!" declared Tee-Bo.

"And sometimes we see the face staring at us—"

"The face of Uncle Rotten Hort."

"Yes," Carlyle went on, "and sometimes we don't. But what puzzles me is—"

"You two never see Uncle Rotten or hear the Horts at the same time," Tee-Bo pointed out. "I thought of that, too."

Carlyle sighed. "At first, I thought it might be because of the stone, but now I know it isn't."

"Stone?" Cam asked quickly. "What stone?"

"That one," she answered, pointing to the pebble he was tossing. "The lapis lazuli."

"This isn't the lapis lazuli," he said impatiently and skipped it across the stream. "It's only a pebble I picked up just now."

"Then," Carlyle said triumphantly, "I'm probably right! You heard the singing when you had it, and so did I—when I had it. The same thing happened with Uncle Rotten Hort. Whoever had the stone could see him!"

Cam stood up and made a sweeping gesture with one hand. "Great reasoning, counselor, but I left the lapis lazuli at home. It's probably on the shelf, where Father put it last night."

"Then I recommend," Tee-Bo cried excitedly, "that the court run home and get it!"

When they reached the house, there, on the kitchen table, was a small bag, with a note from Mother: *Gone to Mrs. Flannella's for tea. Sandwiches in bag.*

"Come on!" cried Cam, who had run into the other room. "I've got the stone!"

"Take our lunch," advised the dog. "We may be gone a long time."

"Shall I put in a bone for you?" Carly asked, picking up the bag.

"No," he replied. "I'm sure Mother made a peanut butter sandwich for me, too."

By the time they had raced back to the woods again, they were hot and sticky. They threw themselves down on the leaves in the cool shade.

"No wonder poor Matchlock almost dried out," observed Cam. "It's hotter than—"

"Blue blazes," suggested Tee-Bo, "a phrase forbidden by Father."

"We might need Matchlock's help again," Cam

went on, "so try and think up some new and terrible spells, Carly."

"I know another one," she replied, "but I'm saving it. Have you seen the face yet?" Cam was carrying the stone.

"No, but I think I can whistle—listen!" He pursed his lips, and a lovely birdcall came forth, low and clear.

He handed the lapis lazuli to his sister. She puckered her lips and at once began whistling such a series of birdcalls that they were enchanted. They traded the precious stone back and forth, until the forest throbbed with music surely never heard in such abundance before.

Even Tee-Bo tried it but had to give up, making a wry face. "It makes my lips tickle," he complained.

"All right, now," Cam ordered a few moments later, when they had reached the falls, "everyone be quiet and listen." A moment later his eyes lit up. "They're singing again!" he whispered, handing the stone to his sister.

Carlyle listened and nodded. "I can hear them as plain as day," she marveled.

"Now you listen," the boy told Tee-Bo, tucking the lapis lazuli firmly under the dog's toes. Tee-Bo hesitated, then tilted his head to one side and did as he was told.

"It's *leery*," he whispered, rolling his eyes at the children.

"You mean *eerie*," Carlyle said, with a look Tee-Bo knew well. "You shouldn't use words unless you know what they mean."

The dog was about to reply, but Cam interrupted. "Let's not argue," he said, "just because we're excited. I'm going to cross over to the other side. Come on."

Large stones had been placed at the top of the falls, where the water spilled between them. They were damp and somewhat slippery, but Tee-Bo and the children had walked over them many times; in a moment, the three of them, stepping carefully, reached the other side. Going down the bank, they stood there staring at the ribbon of water pouring into the pool at their feet. Cam felt in his pocket to make sure the lapis lazuli was there.

"I'm going closer," he told them. "Wait here."

He stepped onto a large boulder and then onto another, the spray from the falls sending a fine mist over him.

"Careful!" warned Tee-Bo, nervously running back and forth.

The boy made his way cautiously from boulder to boulder, until he reached the falls. They saw him reach out to let the spray play over his hand and then bend over to peer behind the dark sheet of water. He remained crouched like this for so long that Tee-Bo began whining impatiently.

"Quiet," Carly begged. "You'll frighten the Horts."

"Frighten *them?*" the dog complained. "How about *us?* We don't even know what they look like!"

"Matchlock said they were friendly to everyone," she reminded him, shivering a little, even though it was so warm.

"That doesn't always include me," he said disconsolately. "I'm different."

At this point, Cam looked back over his shoulder and called to them.

"I've found something! Come on!"

Carlyle grabbed the bag of sandwiches and began making her way over the boulders, Tee-Bo following. When they came to the last boulder, they had to jump to the small spot of damp ground where Cam stood pointing behind the curtain of falling water.

"There's a cave back in there; I'm sure of it," he said. "It could be the way to the country of the Horts."

There was a dark hole in the rocks behind the falls, large enough to step into, if one bent over, and lined thickly with moss, over which water trickled and streamed in rivulets.

Carlyle shivered even harder. "Can you still hear

them?" she whispered. For answer, her brother handed her the stone. Her eyes widened as she listened. "It's much louder, but it's so sad. I wonder what sort of dreadful thing could have happened to them."

"Hah!" snorted Tee-Bo, but quietly. "We'd better think of what dreadful thing might happen to us!"

"I'm going to see where this cave leads to," Cam said firmly. "You can stay here, if you like."

"I'm going, too," Carlyle said quickly, "so don't go too fast!"

Tee-Bo rolled his eyes and shook his head, muttering, "Forevermore!" as he bounded after them.

Bending over, they stepped carefully through the opening, feeling the thick, damp moss covering the solid rock on both sides. It was so dark that at first they could not even see one another and so narrow that, once or twice, they had to turn sideways to squeeze through.

Suddenly Cam spoke. "Look," he said, his voice sounding hollow and echoing from all sides, "we can stand up now."

"I wish we could see," Carlyle whispered. The sound of the falls was far behind them now. Except for a musical trickle of water dripping over rocks somewhere near, there was nothing but their breathing to disturb the deep silence.

"Do you still have the stone?" Carlyle asked.

"It's here," Cam whispered and took it from his pocket. At once a rush of bluish green light flooded the place, revealing the children's astonished faces as they stared at each other.

"Help!" cried Tee-Bo, growling and looking around nervously. "Who did that?"

"Quiet!" Cam commanded. "I don't know."

"It's coming from the lapis lazuli," Carlyle said. "Look!"

A clear, greenish light was pouring from the stone Cam held in his hand, illuminating everything around them. They were standing in a rock grotto, with a smooth rock floor under their feet. The damp rock walls and ceiling were all heavily overgrown with moss, in many places splashing and dripping with water. At their feet lay steps carved from rock, leading downward into a soft gloom, beyond which the light did not penetrate.

Cam didn't hesitate. "Follow me," he said, "and watch your step." The warning was hardly necessary, for the stairs were low and broad and thick with carpetlike moss. At the bottom, they found a rock wall before them, as smooth as glass and reaching from floor to ceiling.

"Good!" Tee-Bo sighed with nervous relief. "Now we can't go any farther, so let's go back."

"We're not going back yet," Cam told him. "We just got here."

He approached the rock wall, holding the stone aloft so that its light played over it, and stared intently ahead.

"This isn't a wall," he informed them. "It isn't a wall at all."

"Then what . . . what is it?" Carlyle's teeth were chattering.

"It's a door."

"But with no doorknob," put in Tee-Bo hastily. "We can't open it, so let's go home."

Suddenly the light vanished, leaving them once more in pitch-blackness.

"I put the stone back in my pocket," Cam explained, "so I could push with both hands. Let's just try it."

"Oh, forevermore!" Tee-Bo declared vexedly. "You two just don't know when you're well-off!"

"Push!" Cam commanded, and they pushed. Even the dog put up his front paws and exerted all his strength.

"Harder!" Cam said, panting.

"No! Don't!" cried Tee-Bo, springing back. "It's opening! It's opening by itself! Get back! Get back!"

In the dark, a muffled, whispering sound could be heard, while a streak of greenish light appeared, widening as the great stone door slowly opened inward. When it had opened fully, the children standing on the threshold gasped with amazement at what lay before them.

5
Outside the Inside

An enormous cavern was exposed to view—so large that its full dimensions could only be guessed at—flooded with luminous green light, with a fine mist in the air, as though a very light rain were falling. Stranger still was the crowd of inhabitants facing them, grouped as though just interrupted in a dance, every face turned toward them and reflecting a mutual astonishment.

For a full thirty seconds, no one moved. Then a figure stepped out of the group and came slowly toward them. It was a full-grown man of delicate build, no higher than Cam's shoulder, clad in a robe of green cloth. Around his neck was a chain bearing a strange medallion.

Approaching the children, he held out a slender hand, as small as a child's, and spoke in a voice of gentle surprise.

"We greet thee, strangers from the Inside, and regret thee had trouble opening the door. Had we known, we would have helped thee. Come out; do come out!"

"Out where?" Cam replied, so confused by what he saw and heard that he hardly knew what he was saying.

"Out's in," Tee-Bo whispered hoarsely, for he was still frightened. "The Horts live Outside."

"Let me introduce myself and my friends," the other went on as the children and the dog came forward timidly, trying not to stare openly but too amazed not to.

Aside from their size and delicate build, the Horts were not unlike other people, though their skins were as waxen as the petals of a gardenia. Their eyes were large and lustrous, as though filled with unshed tears.

"I am known as Courtly Hort," the speaker announced, "and this is my good spouse, Gracious Hort." He indicated a personage smiling quietly at his side. "My daughter, Silken," he continued, turning to an exquisite creature standing next to a young man of stalwart appearance, the tallest of them all, "and this is Curly Hort." Obviously the young man was so named because of the abundance of thick curls crowning his handsome head. "Silken and Curly Hort are affianced," Courtly Hort finished proudly.

"Does that mean that they're bankrupt?" Tee-Bo whispered.

"It means they're engaged to be married," Carlyle whispered back. "Stop growling, Tee-Bo. You'll frighten them."

Stepping forward in her mother's best manner, the little girl held out her hand, which the elder Hort accepted gracefully. "We're happy to meet you, Mr. Courtly Hort, and your family, too." She then made the introductions, ending with, "Tee-Bo is our dog."

Tee-Bo sighed. "That doesn't always put me in the top five hundred, I'm afraid."

"They might not know what a dog is," Carlyle said hastily, "and you could scare them, growling like that."

"We have heard of thee," replied Courtly, addressing the dog and bowing slightly, "from our friend, good Matchlock, who dwells on the Inside by the pond. He speaks well of thee, Dog Tee-Bo."

Tee-Bo's ears stood upright in surprise. "Can he hear me?" he asked, turning to Cam.

Silken began to laugh, with a sound as of tinkling

bells. "Is that so strange? Thee speaks; why should we not hear?"

"It is teatime," Courtly Hort announced then, "and we will be most honored if thee will partake with us."

"Please—we wouldn't want to intrude," Carlyle said, but Gracious Hort would not hear of their doing otherwise and led them toward a stairway leading to a broad shelf cut from the rock wall. They were accompanied by the three jolly musicians who had supplied the music for the dancing. Courtly introduced them as Kluge, Brock, and Camel Hort.

"I used to have a friend on the Inside," Camel remarked, seating himself at the rock table, which was set for tea, "named Fred. But he grew up."

"Was he sick?" asked Tee-Bo, leaping up onto the stone bench beside him.

"Pardon me," replied the other politely. "I said *grew* up."

At this, Curly Hort let out a loud, hearty laugh, and Silken turned her face away to hide a smile.

"Thee is a jolly fellow," Curly laughed, reaching over and patting Tee-Bo, his great eyes sparkling with fun. "We should have met thee long ago."

Gracious Hort was arranging the tea-things, her tiny hands moving so gracefully that the children were fascinated.

"We do hope," she said, "thee will enjoy our fern cakes and trillium tea. A light repast"—her face clouded for a moment, as though something sad had occurred to her—"but supper, of course, comes later."

"Of course, good Gracious," her husband replied, looking at her rather anxiously, "later, to be sure."

For a moment, everyone had looked worried at the mention of supper, but now they all smiled again.

The fern cakes were exceedingly thin and melted in their mouths, leaving a taste of honey, while the trillium tea, pale pink in color, was served in fragile, flower-shaped cups, also pink-tinted.

The children sipped their tea and ate their fern cakes with the utmost care, so as not to break anything. There were only two fern cakes apiece but plenty of tea, which their hostess was quick to pour the instant a cup was emptied, even that of Tee-Bo, who was lapping carefully, wishing he had been given a saucer instead of a cup.

"This will do thee good," Gracious told the children, looking at them with some concern, "for thee have much color. Have thee been ill?"

"Oh, no," both replied, in surprise.

"Not ill?" Silken asked, brushing Carlyle's cheek with a feathery touch. "With such color?"

"Perhaps," her father suggested gravely, "those on the Inside have different complexions. We do not

know," he added, addressing the children, "for we go Inside to the forest only at dark."

"I daresay," his wife put in pleasantly, "we appear quite unusual to thee, too."

"You are very pale," Carlyle replied and then stopped, fearing she sounded rude.

"Oh, thank thee!" Gracious responded, while there were pleased smiles all around, as though a fine compliment had been paid. "We try to look our best."

Though by now there wasn't a single fern cake left, and almost all the trillium tea was gone, too, their hostess asked if she could serve them more. At this, Tee-Bo, completely forgetting that the Horts were well able to hear him speak, said in a roguish voice, meanwhile rolling his eyes, "Yessir! How about some pe-can, pop-nuts, chewing-corn, and gum-dy?"

"Tee-Bo!" both children said together.

The poor fellow, instantly recognizing his error, slid off the bench to the floor, put his head back up to say, "Pardon me!" and went under the table, the picture of mortification.

"We must tell thee something of the Horts," Courtly Hort began gravely, much in the manner of Father when describing the Mongolians, "for it is clear that thee have no knowledge of our customs or our history." So, while Curly and Silken bent their heads down under the table to whisper friendly encouragement to Tee-Bo, without being heard, the elder Hort went on in his quaint and kindly tones.

"The Horts have dwelt here on the Outside for as long as time itself, but no one can say exactly how long time is. Our records start earlier than even the Great Change, when water flowed naturally uphill and the Great Orb on the Inside, which thee call 'Sun,' rose not in the east, as it now does, but in the west. It *set* in the east."

Here Carlyle could not help uttering a word of surprise. "We know about that!" she cried. "Father told us!"

Cam nodded. "From the Bambo Books. How Earth tilted on its axis when the planet Venus came within Earth's orbit—before it was a planet, I think," he ended.

Courtly Hort was nodding with a pleased smile. "All true, all true," he murmured. "Roughly, about thirty-four hundred years past. Yet our horticulture goes back thousands of years before even this remote past. All recorded on stone." He nodded solemnly. "We place our origin, our very first beginnings, in the great Pan Hort, founder and benefactor of our race. Let me show thee."

He led them to the rear of the chamber, to a stone plaque set in the wall. On it was the same inscription as that on the medallion he wore around his neck.

"In our ancient tongue," he explained, "is here written the Golden Rule of the Horts: *View Thy Fellow Hort as in a Mirror, so that if Thee Hurt Him, Thee Wound Only Thyself.*"

They had returned to the table, and the elder Hort was about to resume his narrative, when Tee-Bo jerked up onto his feet, yelping loudly with surprise and pain.

"Who did *that?*" he cried, staring wildly at the Horts about him.

"Did what?" asked Cam.

"Something pulled my tail—hard," replied the dog, with a quick glance over his shoulder at the rock pillar.

"Tee-Bo," Carlyle said, "there's nothing there."

"Well, nothing pulls mighty hard, and if it does it again, nothing's going to feel my teeth in it!" He settled down again gingerly but a moment later jumped up again, leaped off the bench, and ran behind the pillar, growling fiercely. At the same time, a grotesque little figure came bounding into their midst, hopped onto the stone table, and stood there laughing raucously and pointing a finger at the astonished dog, who had stopped short in his pursuit.

"Hee-hee-hee!" snickered the creature in great disdain. "Stay away from me, shaggy monster, or Curly Hort will pound you into a fern cake!"

6
The Great Wet-Stone

While everyone else stared in shocked surprise, Curly Hort rose and addressed the intruder in a voice of reprimand. "Get down from there instantly! Thee must see we have guests."

"Oh, thee—thee—thee!" mimicked the creature, making horrid faces at the other. "When Uncle Rotten Hort returns, he'll chase 'em all away; you'll see! Monsters!" Then he proceeded to make faces at the rest of the group.

The children stared in surprise. The newcomer resembled the other Horts, except that he was shorter and had a wide, turned-up nose, whereas the others' noses were straight and delicate. Also, he wore a long-tasseled cap over hair, as coarse as a hedgehog's, that stuck out all over his head.

"Monsters, monsters, monsters!" he jeered, stamping and slapping his shoes frenziedly on the tabletop.

"Thee must apologize to our guests," Courtly said sternly.

"I never will! I don't have to!" returned the other, jerking his head so that the cap fell over one eye, while the remaining one glared balefully out. "I'm wicked and bad, you know, and Uncle Rotten is as proud of me as he can be!"

At this, Silken rose and, reaching out, placed her delicate hand on the creature's shoulder.

"Wort Hort," she said tenderly, "thee are not bad or wicked. Thee knows this. We have been friends since childhood, thee and Curly Hort and I."

"Sit thee down to tea," Gracious added. "Thee will feel better."

"Oh, I'll take tea! Delicious trillium tea!" Wort Hort declared, skipping across the table and taking a seat next to Silken, whom he crowded uncomfortably. "But I'm still as wicked as can be, and don't you dare say I'm not!"

Courtly shook his head. "Thee, Wort Hort, *thee.* Not *you.*"

"I don't say 'thee' anymore," returned the other

rudely, sipping his tea with loud, smacking noises. "I'm mad, and I belong to the new and mean generation. I'll show you all, I will!"

Meanwhile, Curly Hort, his brows drawn together in stern disapproval, had exchanged places with Silken and now sat next to Wort Hort.

"I want to sit next to Silken!" screamed Wort instantly, shaking a fist at Curly. "You took my place, you big bully!" He jumped up and down on the bench, in a temper tantrum.

"Thee should sit next to a viper to teach thee manners," Curly returned, putting an arm about Silken to protect her.

At this, the little creature's face turned purple with rage. "Silken was supposed to marry up with me! Me! Me!" he screamed, digging his fists into his eyes and kicking at Curly's strong back.

Courtly Hort had risen, his patience having come to an end. "I forbid thee to talk thus of my daughter." Pointing a finger at the frenzied Hort, he added sternly, "Stop this nonsense, or thee must leave."

Wort ran around behind Curly and threw his arms about Silken's neck.

"Protect me, dear Silken! Save me from these cruel monsters! Only thee will I call 'thee,' dear, dear Silken!" He wept tears that fell on the dark gloss of her hair.

Poor Silken blushed scarlet and then turned white. "Wort," said she, with a look so sorrowful it would have melted a heart of stone, "sit thee down next to me if thee will, then, but do be more manful and quiet. Thee are distressing to my parents and our guests."

Wort peeped out slyly from behind Silken's curls.

"Guests!" he squeaked. "Those monsters? Look how big and ugly they are! And I don't want to sit next to you now, Silken; you're a bad thing, and I hate you! I do! I do!" Then he jumped back onto the table, making horrid, leering faces at all of them.

Suddenly he spied something partly concealed under Silken's plate. With a lunge, he darted over and grabbed it, stuffing it into his mouth and devouring it. "Thought I didn't see it, did you?" he jeered. "The last fern cake, and you hid it, you deceitful girl!"

"I . . . I was saving it for Curly," stammered poor Silken, looking as if she were about to cry, "but thee could have had it, had thee asked."

"I don't need to ask!" Wort shouted loudly at her. "Soon I'll have all the fern cakes I want. Uncle Rotten Hort and I will own everything, even the nutmeg trees in the woods—*all of 'em*—and you know why . . . why . . . why? Because we have the Wet-Stone, the Great Wet-Stone, hee-hee-hee, and thee—I mean *you*—won't never see it again! Never!" He danced, snickering and making faces, up and down the length of the table.

Without meaning to, however, the wicked little creature came too close to Tee-Bo, who, with the children, had sat speechless with astonishment at the scene before him. Wort Hort kicked the dog's paw, which was resting on the table, and Tee-Bo, with a roar of surprise, snapped at him, ripping an inch or so of cloth from his pantaloons.

"Ow! Ow! Ow!" screeched the other in terror, real this time. He would have run back to Silken, but Curly put his hand out and tripped him, and Wort fell flat on his face on the table, scattering cups and plates in all directions.

"Thee are not hurt," Courtly Hort told him. "Go now!"

"I'll go! I'll go," screamed Wort, "but I'll listen!"

Jumping from the table, he ran into the dark recesses of the cavern. Gracious and Silken picked up the scattered plates, with Curly's help.

"We must ask thee to pardon our young friend," Courtly said. "He has been badly influenced by his uncle."

"I'd have him for dinner," said Tee-Bo, "browned on both sides."

Gracious sighed deeply, looking at her husband.

"Perhaps thee should explain to our guests."

"I was about to," he returned. "Thee must think all this most unseemly."

"Matchlock said you were in great trouble," Carlyle said, "but he didn't tell us what it was—not one word—because he'd promised not to."

"An excellent fellow!" Their host nodded. "We visited often in the good days, but no more, no more."

"Only because of Wort," put in Curly, "whom thee will not allow me to chastise."

"Let me explain." Courtly surveyed the group, his kindly features much saddened. "The trouble began last summer, when the Great Wet-Stone was stolen by Uncle Rotten Hort. He took it in the dead of night, and its loss was not discovered until the next day. We hunted high and low, throughout the land, and finally concluded that it had been removed to the Inside, where, of course, we could not go."

"Where thee would not permit me to pursue him," Curly added darkly. Silken put her hand in his and patted his shoulder.

"Why can't you go out—I mean *in*—to the woods," asked Cam, "if Uncle Rotten Hort can?"

"Ah, but he has the Wet-Stone with him!" Courtly, turning, gestured to a niche carved in a far wall, carefully draped with diaphanous silver cloth. Below it was an inscription. "That is where the Great Wet-

Stone has stood since time unknown. Concealed within its interior are precious stones of magic properties. Each year we Horts place one stone apiece in our pockets, over our hearts, and then venture into the woods to harvest the nutmeg. Nutmeg, I must now explain, is our staff of life. Because of the disappearance of the Wet-Stone, we could not harvest it this year, and we are running perilously short of food."

"But why can't you go into the woods without the stone?" persisted Cam.

"The Great Orb—to thee, the Sun—would dry us to a crisp in a matter of hours," Curly answered. "Unless," he added significantly, "one were quick and powerful and found the Wet-Stone very soon—which I am certain I could do, were it allowed."

"It has always been so with the Horts," Courtly continued. "We are of a delicate constitution, needing constant vapor in order to exist. That is why we live Outside and venture Inside only to harvest our food for the year."

"Isn't there anything you can do?" asked Carlyle, deep concern in her voice.

Courtly Hort hesitated for a moment and then nodded solemnly, at which Gracious Hort gasped and quickly took one of his hands in her own.

"We must move according to the law of our land," he replied in low tones, as though unwilling to say what he was about to. "The law states clearly that if the Wet-Stone be removed from its niche, by any means whatsoever, it falls to the part of the eldest Hort to effect its recovery—the eldest in this case being I, Courtly Hort."

"And you'll die, Courtly Hort! You'll die!" screeched a hoarse voice, and Wort Hort leaped out of the shadows, jumping around Courtly's chair and pointing at him while he jeered, "You'll die, Courtly Hort! You'll shrivel away to a dried kernel, you will! Kernel Hort! Kernel Hort! Yah, yah, yah!"

Gracious Hort bent her head sadly, turning so that her face was hidden, while Silken broke into sobs, putting her head on Curly's shoulder and letting the tears splash on the front of his robe.

7
Turned to Ice!

Courtly sighed heavily. "They take it very hard." Rising, he placed an arm about his wife's shoulders and helped her to her feet. "We beg thee to excuse us. We have affairs to settle."

When they had left, Silken took her head from Curly's shoulder and began to dry her tears. "I keep forgetting I'm a grown girl," she said.

"Thee are brave," Curly said fondly. "It is I who am cowardly. I should not listen to thy good father but go into the woods after the thief and bring back the Great Wet-Stone."

Silken shook her head sadly. "Thee cannot break

the law of the land, even though thee are strong and brave."

"We must use our wits, then," said Curly.

"Do as I do," remarked Tee-Bo, "and start from scratch."

"This is no time for jokes," Cam told him, frowning disapprovingly.

"It wasn't meant for one," replied the dog. "They've got to start from *somewhere*."

Curly rose, looking stalwart and determined, though he was no taller than Cam. "We must start from *here*, and soon, for in a mere two days, good Courtly must begin his search for the Great Wet-Stone—and this we must prevent, at no matter what cost to us."

Silken explained to the others that her father had been ruler of the Horts up until a year ago but that now all but a few had deserted him, believing he was responsible for the theft, for he had befriended Uncle Rotten Hort and had trusted him, ill-placed as that trust had proved to be.

"Where do you think he's taken the Wet-Stone?" Cam asked.

"Into the woods, of course," both Horts replied at once.

"How big is it?"

"So big," Curley replied, using his hands.

"About the size of a roc's egg? Now, where would he hide something that big? Is it heavy?"

"I have carried it," Curly answered proudly.

"So has the thief," Tee-Bo declared, "and farther than anyone else, apparently."

Cam, his arms folded across his chest, was staring hard at Curly. "Uncle Rotten Hort isn't as tall as you are."

"Nor is he as strong," put in Silken.

Curly looked at the boy strangely. "How would thee know how tall Uncle Rotten Hort is? Thee have not seen him."

"I have!" Carlyle said eagerly.

Cam nodded. "So have I."

"But we are invisible in the woods," Curly insisted. "All Horts are."

The children shook their heads. "Not to us," Cam told him. "We both saw him."

"This is impossible," Curly repeated firmly. "No one ever sees the Horts in the woods. We are invisible. Thee have seen someone else."

But when they described the little man who had followed them and who surely could have been none other than Uncle Rotten Hort, their friends were greatly mystified.

"Thee have seen a Hort in the woods?" Curly kept saying, until Cam suddenly remembered the piece of lapis lazuli in his pocket and, without further ado, showed it to them.

Both Curly and Silken fell silent on seeing it. At length Curly, bending more closely to examine it, asked the boy who had given it to him. He and Silken listened carefully as Cam explained how he had found it on the path to Mrs. Firstpenny's house and how it had first enabled them to hear the voices singing behind the waterfall.

"It is indeed a fragment of the Great Wet-Stone," Curly replied. "They must keep this," he said to Silken, who nodded, "for thy good father would have it this way if he knew. This proves, then, that the Great Wet-Stone was taken through the woods—but it does not mean that it is still there."

"If it has been taken out of the woods," poor Silken said brokenly, "it would be of no use for my father to search for it. His sacrifice would be in vain." She sank down on the bench, weeping bitterly, her tears floating about her in a mist that mingled with the vapors that moved throughout the great cavern like a fog.

There was a long pause, broken at length by Curly, who spoke in a troubled voice. "Is the Inside, then, quite a . . . quite a large place? Does it cover many miles? Seas and mountains?"

Cam nodded. "It's very big."

"And would take, then, far more than two days' travel to cover entirely?"

"On foot?" asked the boy.

"On foot," repeated the other.

"Much more than two days. More than two years, even."

"Then we are lost, indeed, for no Hort can live on the Inside for more than two days without the aid of the Great Wet-Stone."

"I'll gladly give you my piece of it," Cam offered, holding the lapis lazuli out to him, but Curly shook his head.

"Thee speak well, but it can never be. Once a particle breaks away from the whole, its powers fade. Though it has enabled thee to see and hear what no other from the Inside has yet seen or heard, to a Hort it has no power. It must be whole. No," he ended with a sigh, "thee cannot help us, and I do not know who can."

Curly Hort pronounced these words so solemnly that the children fell silent, and for several minutes there was no sound in the cavern but the delicate sobbing of poor Silken and the whisper of vapory mists. Then Cam spoke up suddenly.

"Tee-Bo, what are you doing?"

"I'm sh-shivering!" the dog snapped back, somewhat cross because he felt so bad about the Horts.

"I'm cold, and I'm sh-shivering."

His coat was damp, with drops of water clinging to it like diamonds, and his chin whiskers trembled as he shook all over.

"I'm c-cold, too," Carlyle admitted, her teeth chattering. She shook her head as she spoke, and the watery vapor flew about her in a misty veil. Even her clothes were damp, and water was soaking through her shoes and socks.

Cam looked down at his garments. "Why am I dry and comfortable?" he asked in surprise. "I didn't realize it was cold."

"It is the Wet-Stone," Curly said, turning from Silken to stare at him. "Its powers will ebb and flow before they fade entirely."

"I wish it could be of some use to you," the boy sighed.

"We must use our wits," Curly replied quietly, "for now they are all that is left to us."

"My wits are frozen," Tee-Bo remarked at this point. "I'm so cold I may never thaw out again, and look at Carlyle! She's beginning to frost over!"

"Carly!" the boy cried, looking at his sister in dismay. "Take this!" He thrust the lapis lazuli into her hand, having to force it between her stiff fingers. It was several moments before she could speak and several more before her clothes began to dry.

Now it was Cam who shivered and shook as the damp vapors saturated him. "P-Pretty s-soon I won't be able to t-talk," he said through his chattering teeth.

"Thee must go at once," Curly said, his voice alarmed, "for it is evident thee cannot withstand our climate any more than we can withstand yours."

Tee-Bo was now in such a state of chill that he could do absolutely nothing. A tip of his tongue, protruding between his teeth, was frozen like a frosty pink icicle.

"Poor Tee-Bo!" cried Carlyle, running to him. "Cam, pick him up and carry him out! He's frozen solid!"

But Cam was now so cold himself that he could not stir. He remained rooted to the spot, his eyes as big as saucers.

"Give Cameron the stone," Curly ordered, "and, by passing it one to the other, leave quickly by yonder door!"

"What about Tee-Bo?" the little girl cried, hastening to do as he had bidden.

"I shall carry the poor beast and follow thee," Curly assured her, and, bending over, he lifted the dog carefully, for he was truly frozen and as brittle as glass. The children hurried to the cavern door and pulled it open, Cam still shivering and dripping, for he had not fully recovered. Curly Hort followed at their heels, stepping cautiously, knowing that if he should stumble and drop his precious burden, poor Tee-Bo could be smashed into a thousand pieces!

8
How to Capture a Hort

Shivering, with chattering teeth and dripping clothes, the children soon reached the top of the moss-grown stairway, looking back meanwhile to make sure the others were not far behind.

By the time Curly Hort had reached their side, the dog was beginning to thaw out. "Thee will be all right now," the Hort told him as he placed him gently on the rock floor and stroked his fur reassuringly. Tee-Bo's eyes were rolling in his head as the water ran off him, and he swallowed, with a gulp, the icicle that had formed on his tongue.

"F-Forevermush!" was all he could say, because he

had a mouthful of ice, but Curly accepted that as his thanks.

"I am forbidden to go farther with thee," he told them, "but thee can find the way easily." He turned to retrace his steps.

"Oh," Carlyle cried out to him, "you mustn't think we won't help you!"

"We'll come back," Cam called, "and find a way to get the Great Wet-Stone!"

"Tell Silken not to worry!" Carly added.

The Hort waved, smiled sadly, and turned toward the entrance. He paused. "Thee would do well to stay away from Uncle Rotten Hort," he warned, "for he is much given to cruel mischief."

A moment or two later, the three emerged from the cave into the bright sunshine of a summer day, making their way over the boulders to the sandy beach beyond.

"Yah! Yah! Hoo-hoo-hoo!" screamed Cam, rolling over and over on the hot sand, picking it up and rubbing it between his fingers and throwing it in the air, not even caring if it showered down on him. His sister followed suit, pulling off her shoes and socks and digging her bare toes in the sand.

Tee-Bo, meanwhile, had taken to rolling over and over, scattering leaves and sand in all directions and grunting his relief and pleasure, for there were no words to fit the occasion—not even for an educated fellow like Tee-Bo!

"I'll never complain about the heat again!" he declared when he had finally tired himself and stood up to shake off the leaves and sand.

"Whew!" Cam whistled in relief as the hot sun streamed over him. "Now I know what Father meant when he said that we just take the sun for granted and what a great sight it would be to see it coming up over the mountains in the east for the very first time!"

"Don't say such things!" Tee-Bo shuddered, and for a moment all three were silent, thinking how strange Earth would be without the big yellow orb that everybody took so much for granted.

"Well," Cam said briskly, "now all we have to do is think of a way to get the Great Wet-Stone away from Uncle Rotten Hort."

"First we have to find him," Carlyle reminded him, "and we don't have much time—only two days, Curly said."

"We'll search the woods right now, then."

"Can't we go home now and start tomorrow?" Tee-Bo begged. "I have a big hollow place inside me, where my dinner ought to be."

But the children would not hear of it, and, reminding him of how hungry the Horts must be without the nutmeg that was their staff of life, they set out, followed by Tee-Bo, to search the woods for any sign of the wicked Hort or the Great Wet-Stone itself.

By the time the sun was sinking below the horizon, they had searched all the trees and all the fallen logs and all the likely and unlikely spots where the Great Wet-Stone might have been hidden, without so much as turning up a clue.

"We still have two days," Cam said determinedly. "We'll get up early tomorrow and start looking again."

That night the children had strange dreams. Cam thought he was fighting a dragon and, leaping out of bed, grabbed up his bedroom slipper and walked straight into the bathroom door. Carlyle dreamed she was back in the Hort country, and Mother said later that she distinctly heard her scream, "Look out, Retort!" but what she had really said was "Look out, Wort Hort!" for she had dreamed that Uncle Rotten Hort was chasing his nephew up and down rocky tunnels, holding the Great Wet-Stone in one hand and threatening to toss it at him. Even Tee-Bo murmured and yelped in his sleep, which made Father declare that it had been a "night for the banshees" and that they should have "only one piece of pie tonight."

The sun rose early, and the day dawned hot and still. As soon as breakfast was over and Father had left for the University in Old Bessie, Mother announced she was going to Mrs. Flanella's to do a sketch of her old Spode teapot, which had been in the family for four generations.

"It's more than two hundred years old, and she's sure it's going to break any day now," Mother explained. "I wouldn't want to live with a teapot that caused me as much worry as that one does."

Tee-Bo stood up, stretching and yawning, as the children came out onto the porch. "Any ideas?" he asked.

Cam shook his head, and Carlyle's face was gloomy. "I thought of a hundred things that wouldn't work."

"We need only one plan," said Cam, in his practical way, "and it's got to work, whatever it is."

They moved rather disconsolately along the river road and were soon on the path to Farrow's Pond. Birds were singing on all sides, and the sky was deep blue. The fragrance of willows and water drifted through the air toward them. At any other time, they would have skipped or run merrily through the woods or just stood there listening to the many voices of wild things, but today they had only one thing in mind: to find the Great Wet-Stone and save the Horts from starvation.

After searching for an hour or two, without success, they sat down to rest, dusting the leaves and stickers from their clothing. Tee-Bo lay at their feet, panting, his bright eyes fixed on them. A bird's call came to them from the bushes, low and sweet. Without thinking, Cam rounded his lips and answered back, in exact imitation of the wild birdcall.

"I guess the lapis lazuli hasn't lost its power yet," his sister said, somewhat enviously. Cam at once handed the stone to her, and when a birdsong floated toward them again, Carlyle imitated it, though ordinarily she wasn't a very apt whistler. They had been amusing themselves for several moments in this manner, when suddenly Tee-Bo let out a yelp of excitement and jumped up.

"I have an idea!" he exclaimed, seeing that they thought he had been stung by a bee. "An idea that just might work!" He sat upright before them, his chin whiskers doing a dance.

Cam grunted, while Carlyle just looked at Tee-Bo mournfully. "It probably would have to be a miracle," she sighed.

"Well, don't turn it down until you've heard it, at least," the dog said indignantly. "Cam," he went on, dropping his voice to a whisper, "you can imitate different sounds, can't you, like Matchlock's voice and these birdcalls you've been doing?"

"Why are you whispering?" the boy returned irritably. "No one's here but us."

Tee-Bo gave him a long look. "How do we know? How do we know," he continued slowly and with great emphasis, "that Uncle Rotten Hort isn't nearby, listening to every word we're saying?"

The children looked at each other. Then Cam said, "But whoever had the stone would see him."

"Please whisper!" the dog insisted. "You wouldn't see him if he kept out of sight, now, would you?"

"No, we wouldn't," Cam replied guardedly, this time remembering to keep his voice down. "You're absolutely right, Tee-Bo."

"You mean, you think he's close enough to hear us?" Carlyle whispered, looking about anxiously.

"Try not to look concerned," the dog urged. "We don't want that dreadful Hort to know that one of us can see him or that we even think he might be near. Just act casual, even though it's hard." And to show his unconcern, Tee-Bo tried to yawn, failed, and swallowed a gnat.

"So much for that," said he, grimacing. "Now, hear my plan and give me your opinion: We'll hide in the forest, all three of us, each in a different place but fairly close together, and just hope Uncle Rotten Hort doesn't catch us hiding. Then, Cam, you must imitate that ugly little creature, Wort Hort. Cry just like Wort Hort does, so his uncle will think he's in terrible danger and rush out to rescue him. See?"

"See what?" the boy demanded, scowling worse than before. Carlyle just stared at Tee-Bo blankly.

"Oh, forevermore," exclaimed the dog impatiently, "you'll be able to see him because you'll have the stone, and you can catch him! Tie him up and make him tell where he hid the Great Wet-Stone!"

Since the children said not a word, the dog went around in a circle and then sat down in the same place.

"Think about it, anyway," he sighed, "unless you can think of something better!"

"Curly said to keep away from him—remember?" Cam said slowly, thinking deeply.

"He isn't any bigger than you are, Cam," his sister reminded him, her voice beginning to sound hopeful, "and he's sort of . . . of puny."

"What does that mean?" asked Tee-Bo, but they ignored him.

"He might . . . bite," Cam said.

"He's not a *dog*," Carlyle objected quickly.

"Well, thanks a lot!" Tee-Bo muttered.

The little girl hastened to apologize, then turned back to Cam. "I can help you, Cam, once you get hold of him!"

"And I'll growl something awful," the dog assured them.

Cam shook his head, still looking doubtful. "What

if someone passes by? Think how I'll look, hanging on for dear life to something that isn't even there!"

"Oh, *potatoes!*" exclaimed Carlyle. "How often do we see anybody near Farrow's Pond? Never!"

"All right," Cam answered reluctantly, "I guess we have to try."

The other two regarded him anxiously.

"Are you sure you can sound like Wort Hort?" Carlyle asked.

"You just listen! But come on; let's find a place to hide!"

9
Too Long in the Woods

At Cam's suggestion, they first settled on a likely place to hide, deep in the woods, and then separated, taking different paths far enough apart to confuse the wily Hort if he should try to follow.

Carlyle made herself invisible behind a clump of bushes. Tee-Bo, having arrived first, lay on his belly against a fallen tree and was hidden by its branches, while Cam crept quietly over a shortcut and crouched low behind a large boulder, near the others. They had agreed to wait a short interval after taking their hiding places, and now, as the minutes ticked by, the forest grew more and more silent, until even a falling leaf could be heard.

Carlyle, who happened to be sitting in a bed of stickers, was beginning to fidget, when suddenly such a caterwauling rang through the forest that she jumped in spite of herself.

"Oh, leave me alone! Monster! Monster! Monster!" called the voice, in a wail of rage and fear. "Oh, help me, Uncle Rotten Hort! Help! Help! Help!"

There was no mistaking *that* voice. It was Wort Hort's shrill squeak, and poor Carlyle's heart thumped in dismay as she crouched in the bushes. What had brought him to the forest just in time to ruin their plan, and, worse yet, what terrible thing was after him to make him scream like that? She was so frightened that she hid her eyes with her hands and put her head down on her knees, so she wouldn't be tempted to look.

Wort Hort continued to squeal, his cries growing more pitiful. "Get away from me, big, ugly thing! Don't touch me! Don't come any nearer! Uncle Rotten Hort, save me! Save me! Help!"

Carlyle couldn't stand it another minute. Leaping to her feet, she dashed across the sand, almost running over her brother, who was rolling on the ground, his face red and his arms thrashing out wildly.

"Now, you stop!" he was saying. "You just stop wriggling and sit still!"

As she watched in amazement, he brought his hands together and assumed a peculiar position, half off the ground, coming to rest with a sigh and a grunt of satisfaction. Then he saw his sister, and a big grin spread over his face.

"I've got him, Carly! It worked! I've got Uncle Rotten Hort, and he's so mad he's *sputtering*, but I guess you can't see him or hear him— Hold still there, sir! Hold still, or I'll have to sit on you!"

Tee-Bo now crept cautiously near and surveyed the scene, his fur bristling.

"You're *sitting* on him?" he asked, walking around and sniffing the ground, so as not to step on the Hort if he really was there.

"Not yet," the boy answered, "but if I have to, I will! And I'll sit hard, too!" This last was for the benefit of the Hort, who, from time to time, was attempting to escape.

"But where's Wort Hort?" Carlyle asked in a bewildered tone.

"Carly, that was my voice! I told you I could do it!"

The boy remained in the same bent position, his hair tousled and hanging over his eyes. For a moment, no one spoke. Then Carlyle asked timidly, "Is he very big?"

"Naw!" Cam tossed his head scornfully. "He's not

as big as Curly Hort, and he's skinnier than Wort Hort. Right now, he's stopped wiggling, and he's threatening either to drop me into a cauldron of boiling oil or to braid me into a rag rug for his grandmother."

"Oh, dear," Carlyle moaned, "this is awful!"

"Oh, I don't mind!" her brother replied cheerfully. "I could hold him down for a week!"

Tee-Bo was looking thoughtful. "You might have to, boy, if you don't get him to tell us where the Great Wet-Stone is."

"Right," Cam agreed, wriggling somewhat to get a firmer hold on his victim. "Now, Uncle Rotten Hort, we won't let you go until you tell us where the Great Wet-Stone is. We know you have it."

"Don't hurt him," said Carlyle, staring anxiously, though, of course, neither she nor the dog could see the Hort. This advice proved to be unnecessary, however, for their wily victim was not to be as easy prey as they thought. After fifteen minutes of demanding and scolding, Cam had to admit not only that the wicked Hort had no intention of giving up his secret but also that he was not sure how much longer he would be able to hold him.

"If you could see him," he complained to the others, "you could help me!"

Tee-Bo growled, "If I could see him, I'd bite him!"

"Maybe I could get the stone out of your pocket," Carlyle suggested hesitantly, for she was hoping she wouldn't have to look at the wicked Hort at all.

"Nope." Her brother shook his head, his face grim. "I have to see him. He'll get away if I don't."

For several moments, they remained deep in thought, until at length it became plain that the boy was beginning to lose his grip.

"He's slippery!" he exclaimed in vexation. "He's about as slippery as an eel! No, you don't! Sit still!"

"Tell you what," Tee-Bo said, his chin whiskers nervously dancing. "Get the Hort's stone away from him. He's got to have one on him, or he couldn't live in the woods, remember?"

Cam fidgeted and scowled more than ever. "Where would it be?"

"Probably around his neck on a chain," Carlyle said. "Silken told me all the Horts have one."

A minute later, Cam let out a yell, and then something fell on the ground at Carlyle's feet.

"He tried to bite me!" Cam yelled. "Pick it up, Carly!"

The little girl bent quickly and picked up the medallion from where it had fallen. As she did so, she saw the puny figure of Uncle Rotten Hort sitting nearby, her brother sitting on his legs and holding a tight grip on his hands.

"Now you've killed me," Uncle Rotten Hort squealed in grievous tones, "for I shall die without my medallion!"

For a moment, Carlyle just stared. It was hard to believe that anyone the same height as her brother could be so thin and so light in weight. The Hort had the same high forehead as all the others and was quite bald, except for a fringe of hair in a circle on top of his head. His eyes were narrow and mean, and his face was deeply wrinkled in furrows of hatred and vexation. He hadn't the gentle voice of the Horts, either; his was rasping and sounded like chicken bones going down the garbage disposal.

"Mr. Rotten Hort," Carlyle addressed him as soon as she recovered from the surprise of seeing him, for until now she'd had only glimpses of him half-hidden by foliage, "how could you ever do such a terrible thing to your friends?"

Her tones were so reproachful that the puny little man began to cough and clear his throat impatiently. Then, with a quick jerk of his head, he replied, "Justified, completely justified! They deserved it! They're beasts!"

"Oh, how can you say that?" cried Carlyle, with tears shining in her eyes.

"It's quite true, my dear," the crafty little man replied, eyeing her carefully. "My nephew Wort was supposed to be affianced to Silken, the daughter of our ruler, and what happened? That ugly fellow Curly stepped in and ruined my nephew's plans—I mean, his future."

"Why, not a word of that is true!" the little girl answered indignantly. "Silken and Curly Hort are engaged because they want to be engaged, and Wort is their childhood friend!"

Uncle Rotten Hort sniffed scornfully, but before he could reply, Cam said calmly, "Besides, this doesn't justify stealing the Great Wet-Stone. Their lives depend on it, and now you've stolen it."

"Oh," retorted the Hort crossly, "I only intend to keep it until Courtly and Gracious come to their senses. In a matter of days, they'll see it my way, mark my words, and then I'll return the Great Wet-Stone and my nephew and Silken will be married. It's a matter of state affairs, and busybody children—if that's what you're supposed to be—shouldn't go sticking their noses into Horts' affairs!"

"What's he saying?" asked Tee-Bo, who could only hear one side of the conversation.

"He's making excuses," Cam answered, "like we do when we're late for dinner."

"He's also trying to blame the other Horts for what he's done," Carlyle added, "and saying he'll keep the Wet-Stone until Silken promises to marry Wort—

which she'll never do, ever!"

"Show me his leg, and I'll teach him a lesson or two!" Tee-Bo asserted, growling and pawing the ground until the wicked Hort's hair stood up on top of his long head.

"Keep that creature away from me!" he squealed. Terrified, he began to struggle so hard that the children knew something had to be done to keep him from making his escape.

"Take your hair ribbon," Cam told his sister, "and tie his wrists together—tight." When this was done, the boy took a length of cord from his pocket and tied the Hort's ankles together firmly. At last he sat back to rest.

Tee-Bo was watching with great interest. "Good. Now I know right where he is," the dog declared, for the ribbon and the cord were plainly visible. "Just tell the old rascal that he'd better behave himself, or I'll take care of him!"

By this time, it was late afternoon, and they still had no idea where the Great Wet-Stone was hidden. Tee-Bo took the children aside so they could talk without being overheard.

"We have only one day left," he reminded them. "If you can't make him talk, I'll have to—painful as that may be to all parties," he added.

"Oh, dear," Carlyle said, shaking her head. "Could

we just threaten to leave him tied up all night in
the woods?"

"That wouldn't work," Cam said firmly. "Wort
Hort might come out and untie him." He sighed and
then, with a plaintive look at the others, added, "I
don't know what to do. I'm only a boy, and I'm not
supposed to browbeat old gentlemen."

"Uncle Rotten Hort isn't an old gentleman at
all—" Carlyle began and then stopped short, her gaze
fixed on the figure of the Hort. "Why, look at him,"
she cried. "He's turning brown!"

As they ran over to the Hort, Tee-Bo let out a yelp.
"I can see him, too! At least, I see two skinny legs
and nothing else. Are those *his?*"

To their horror, Uncle Rotten Hort, grimacing
with shame, covered his face with his hands and began rocking back and forth, moaning and groaning.

"What's the matter?" cried Tee-Bo, greatly concerned. "Did he run off and leave his legs behind?"

"No, but they're turning brown," Carlyle told him
hastily. "What's the matter?" she asked the Hort,
while she and Cam stared at him anxiously.

"Now you've done it," their captive said in a quav-
ering voice. "You've taken my stone from me, you
cruel monsters, and before nightfall, I shall turn as
crisp as an autumn leaf and wither away! Oh, me!
Oh, poor, poor me!"

10
A Leg of Mutton?

"Why can't you live for two days without your stone?" demanded Cam, eyeing him suspiciously, while Carlyle explained to Tee-Bo what was happening. "Courtly Hort said *he* could."

"I've been too long in the woods already," the other replied, commencing to whimper again. "Now see what your wicked mischief has done!"

"Serves him right!" the dog said with deep satisfaction. "Let him turn brown all over and blow away!"

"All right, Uncle Rotten Hort," Cam told him, with great finality, "now you can see what your trickery has done. All the Horts will die—and you, too—

just because you won't tell us where you've hidden the Great Wet-Stone."

"I can't, I can't, I can't," moaned the old fellow. Peeping between his fingers at his legs, he saw that they were, indeed, becoming leathery and brown, and at this he shrieked all the louder.

"You'd better tell us," Cam ordered sternly, "or we'll just walk off—we have to go home to dinner, anyway—and when we come back tomorrow or the day after, you'll just be another leaf blowing in the wind!"

"And we won't even know which one," Carlyle added. "What a shame."

"But I can't! I can't!" cried the Hort, wriggling in real distress now.

"Come on, then." Cam turned and began to walk away. "We have to get home before dark. Pleasant dreams, Uncle Rotten Hort!"

They had taken only a step or two when the old fellow cried out to them. "Stop! Come back!" he called in desperation. "You've got to help me! You can't leave me like this!"

"Then tell us where the Great Wet-Stone is," Cam said.

"I . . . I can't tell you," the Hort replied, looking at his leathery hands in dismay. "I hid it, I confess. I stole it, and I hid it, but it's not there now. I don't know where it is. Somebody's taken it."

"Where did you hide it?" Cam demanded.

"In that old barn yonder," the other answered with a gulp. "In the soft hay in that old barn, but someone took it."

"Whose barn?"

"That old lady's barn. On the edge of the woods."

"Mrs. Firstpenny's barn!" Carlyle exclaimed, adding quickly, "So you were the one who played all those tricks on her!"

"She must have found it," Uncle Rotten Hort went on in grieved tones, "after I'd hidden it so cleverly, too! Oh, what a meddlesome busybody! Oh, what trouble she has caused me! And now look at me! Oh! Oh! Oh!"

"Now what?" demanded Tee-Bo, running around in circles excitedly. "If it's in the barn, let's go get it!"

"He hid it in the barn," the boy explained, "but it's gone."

"He thinks Mrs. Firstpenny has it," Carlyle added.

Cam stared anxiously at the sky. The sun had set, and long shadows were darkening the woods.

"Carly, you'd better go see Mrs. Firstpenny. I'll stay here."

The little girl looked at the Hort, whose skin was beginning to resemble leather all over, while the creature glared back at her spitefully.

"You big ugly things," he rasped at them both. "I'll get even with you, I will!"

"You'd better let him have this back," Carlyle decided, handing the medallion to her brother. "We don't want him to get any crisper. He looks like—"

"Dried venison?" asked Tee-Bo, licking his lips.

Cam agreed to let the Hort have the medallion for short intervals only, on the condition that he speak respectfully and stop threatening them, and Carlyle left them, hurrying down the path to Mrs. Firstpenny's house.

The first sight that met her eyes was the pleasant old lady herself, standing in the front garden talking with a dark, foreign-looking man in boots and work clothes.

"Byron," the little girl heard her saying as she came up to them, "you must borrow your cousin Hurdle's camera. Bring him with you, and we'll have tea."

Mrs. Firstpenny was wearing her best white apron —the one with flowers embroidered on it. In her hair was a comb with three fine cameos in it, which had belonged to her great-grandmother and which she wore only on festive occasions.

"Hello, my dear!" Mrs. Firstpenny called out the moment she saw her. "Your mother has only just phoned to ask if you were here. Have you met Mr.

Chesapeake? He's our blacksmith. Byron, this is Carlyle, Dr. McRae's little girl."

Mrs. Firstpenny had a spot of rosy pink on each cheek, and her eyes were shining. Byron Chesapeake, the blacksmith, bowed to Carlyle as best he could, being a pudgy fellow, and then asked to be excused, since he had more horses to shoe.

"Do come in," the old lady urged as soon as he had left. "I've just had Heavingham shod, and Mr. Chesapeake and I were having a little talk—about something very exciting, as you will soon see."

"I mustn't stay," Carlyle said, following her inside the house.

Mrs. Firstpenny nodded, her round face beaming. "I'll not keep you a moment. Just long enough for a cookie—and something else."

She held out the jar, and Carlyle took a fudge cookie. "Thank you very much," she said.

"And now, come in here, my dear." The old lady's voice trembled with excitement. "I want you to see what Mrs. Firstpenny has found!"

She led Carlyle into the dining room where the heavy draperies were drawn across the windows. Even in the semidarkness, the little girl saw it instantly and knew exactly what it was. On Mrs. Firstpenny's best table, a large glass bowl had been placed, and in the bowl, carefully set on folds of protective

red velvet, was an oval, highly polished stone as large as the egg of the fabled roc, standing upright on its smaller end. In the dusky twilight of the room, it shed a glow that filled every corner with a soft, blue green light in ripples of moving color.

"Oh!" cried Carlyle, hardly daring to breathe. "What—" Then she stopped, afraid to ask what it was.

"Mr. Chesapeake is borrowing his cousin Hurdle's camera to take a picture of it," said Mrs. Firstpenny, staring as if she couldn't take her eyes off it. "He thinks it might have prehysterical value. I think that's what he said."

Carlyle stared at the Great Wet-Stone. "It's beautiful," she said.

"It's beautiful," Mrs. Firstpenny said dreamily. "It's the most beautiful thing I ever owned. Who would think, really, that such a thing would happen to Mrs. Firstpenny?"

"Well . . ." Carlyle said. "Well. . . ."

"Oh, dear me," cried the old lady, "here I am keeping you, and you must get home! Here, take a cookie for your brother." She pressed two cookies into Carlyle's hand and added a third. "One for Tee-Bo, too. I declare, I'm so flustered with my new treasure that I'm just not myself. Tsk, tsk. I wish Mr. Firstpenny were here to see this. Now, hurry, dear."

"Is it late?" asked Carlyle, hurrying to the door.

The old lady beamed at her.

"Tomorrow the poultry commissioner is coming," she half whispered, as though it were a precious secret. "The head poultry commissioner himself! To Mrs. Firstpenny's! I've called him, and he's promised to come!" Suddenly a worried expression crossed her face. "I hope it doesn't *hatch* before he gets here! Do you think it might?"

"Might *hatch?*" repeated the little girl anxiously.

"No, of course it won't!" returned Mrs. Firstpenny happily, and she waved good-bye from the porch, sighing with happiness.

Carlyle hurried through the woods as fast as possible, tears stinging her lids. *Oh, dear,* she thought, *poor Mrs. Firstpenny's found the Horts' Great Wet-Stone, and she thinks it's an egg, maybe a roc's egg, and she doesn't know the Horts will die without it! Oh, dear!*

By the time she reached Cam's side, her tears were falling fast, and when she had related her story and told Cam and Tee-Bo how proud and happy the old lady was with her discovery, they looked grave and understood why she was so upset.

"This *is* a pickle," said Cam, frowning.

"A cucumber pickle," added Tee-Bo, who hated pickles.

"And she's phoned the poultry commissioner to come out and look at it, and he's coming tomorrow!"

"The poultry commissioner!" echoed the boy and the dog together.

"And Byron Chesapeake is coming to take a picture of it, and, for all we know, Mother and Father and the whole town, because Mother phoned, and we have to get home!"

"I know," Cam said. "It's getting dark."

"What are we going to do with His Royal Venison?" asked Tee-Bo. They were standing a little distance from the Hort, who could not hear them.

"He looks better," Carlyle observed. "He's getting back his silvery."

"His disposition hasn't improved," sighed her brother. "I sometimes think he *ought* to wither away."

"What shall we do with him?"

"There's nothing to do but leave him right where he is, until tomorrow."

"I'll second the motion," Tee-Bo agreed quickly.

"Leave him all night in the woods?" Carlyle protested. "Oh, no!"

"He has his medallion. He'll be all right."

"Well," cried Carlyle, "how would you like to be tied up all night alone in the woods?"

"For Pete's sake," her brother answered, "all right;

Tee-Bo can stay with him."

Much to their surprise, the dog was regarding them with a look of strong reproach.

"You mean you won't stay in the woods, either?" demanded Cam.

"I didn't say I wouldn't," the dog answered, his chin whiskers beginning to tremble, "but it seems to me—" He gulped and swallowed once or twice, turning his face away.

"Now what's wrong?" Cam asked. "All I said was—"

"It seems to me," interrupted Tee-Bo, talking very fast, "that it's strange to care about a wicked Hort staying all night in the woods but not to worry one bit about your very own dog."

"But you've spent lots of nights in the woods!" retorted the boy.

"Not watching a Hort that can't be seen!" Tee-Bo snapped back.

"Hah!" Cam shoved his hands in his pockets and stared at the dog in exasperation. "I guess he'll just have to stay here alone!"

"That's cruel!" Carlyle declared, stamping her foot on the leafy ground. "And, besides, Cam, he could get away! Or Wort Hort could free him, and then he might steal the Great Wet-Stone all over again!"

"And tomorrow's our last day," finished Tee-Bo,

nodding his head warningly.

"Oh, for Pete's *sake!*" Cam scolded, in a loud tone. He stared at them for a moment, letting his breath out in a long sigh. Suddenly he marched over to the Hort and, without a word, reached down and picked him up as easily as he would a baby, a look of supreme disgust on his face.

"There's only one thing left to do," he informed them. "We'll take him home with us and keep him all night!"

With this he turned and began to make his way along the path for home, with Uncle Rotten Hort screaming at the top of his lungs, "Don't take me out of the woods, you idiots! I'll dry up like a leg of mutton!"

11
A Most Discouraging Captive

The Hort's screams grew so persistent that Cam presently stopped and begged him to quiet down. This served only to make him screech the louder, protesting piteously that he would turn into a leg of mutton before they even reached the edge of the woods.

"You'll do nothing of the sort!" the boy replied in somewhat of a temper. "We'll give back your medallion presently. You know you won't dry up, so stop bawling!"

Uncle Rotten Hort continued screaming, however, while Cam, his cheeks red with exasperation, marched on, a deep scowl on his face.

Carlyle, who now had charge of the Hort's medallion, moved up beside him. "From in back, it looks like you're carrying a little boy," she said with a giggle.

"A crybaby, you mean," her brother said. "I wish he'd be quiet, even if we are the only ones who can hear him."

They both had to yell to be heard over the Hort's shrill cries.

"If you're not quiet," Cam shouted, "I'll have to muzzle you! And I'll do it, too!"

Uncle Rotten Hort stopped in the middle of a scream.

"*Muzzle* me!" he repeated, after a moment. Then he looked up craftily at the boy. "You wouldn't dare!"

"Oh, yes, he would!" Carlyle told him. "Don't think he wouldn't!"

"Really? *Muzzle* me?" the Hort said again, a look of such terror darting into his eyes that the others knew he didn't understand the term and thought it some unspeakable form of punishment. "I will not scream out, then," he said finally, "if thee will promise not to hurt me."

Carlyle looked surprised at the "thee."

"Slip of the tongue!" snapped the old fellow, as rudely as possible.

"We won't *hurt* you," Cam declared, now walking with a rather jaunty air, since things were going better, "as long as you behave yourself and keep—"

"A civil tongue in my head," finished the Hort testily. "I know; you've said it more than enough times already."

Tee-Bo came up behind Cam now, looking a little shamefaced at his refusal to remain all night in the woods.

"Hi," he said to the boy in a cheerful tone, but Cam did not reply.

"Is he heavy?" the dog asked, in the polite way people will who have quarreled and want to make up.

"Not in the least!" replied Cam coldly, marching on. They had passed Farrow's Pond and reached the bridge.

"There's something I ought to bring to your attention," Tee-Bo said nervously, trotting by his side. "About the Hort, I mean."

"Don't bother," said Cam, not turning his head.

"Well, forevermore," Tee-Bo retorted, "you don't need to act as if you'd swum the English Channel!"

"Maybe I did!" Cam's expression showed that he was aware he had made a stupid remark.

Carlyle looked inquiringly at Tee-Bo. "What's the matter?"

Tee-Bo drew her attention to the Hort's two thin

little legs as they dangled from the boy's arms. "See what I mean? They'll show!"

Beneath the silver transparency of the skin, the Hort's legs were once more beginning to turn brown and leatherlike.

Carlyle ran up and placed the medallion quickly about the Hort's neck, before he might notice his condition. "You should have listened to Tee-Bo!" she whispered to Cam, which made the boy turn around with a whistle and a grin that ended that quarrel very quickly.

"What will we do with him?" Carlyle asked nervously as they neared home.

"Put him in my room, I guess," Cam answered. They hadn't really looked this far ahead and were now very ill at ease, afraid of whom they might see, though they knew that the Hort, so long as he remained silver, was invisible to everyone else.

"Do I look all right?" Cam asked self-consciously, pausing in front of their house.

"Your arms look strange," Tee-Bo said. "Could you hold them closer to you?"

"Ow!" the Hort screamed. "You're squeezing me to death!"

"Sorry!" Cam reached the front door, opened it, and flew across the hall. Just as he reached the foot of the stairway, he looked up, and there was Father at the top, staring down at him.

"Good evening, son," Father said heartily. "Had a pleasant day in the forest?"

"Very pleasant, Father," the boy replied, hesitating. He knew how awkward he must look with his arms held that way. Father came slowly down the stairs.

"Have you hurt your hands?" he asked, looking critically at them.

"Oh, what a big, ugly thing *that* one is!" cried Uncle Rotten Hort, who had been clinging to Cam in fright. "Don't let him touch me!"

"Stop screaming!" Cam hissed between clenched teeth. At this moment, Mother appeared in the hallway below.

"Well, it's time you two arrived home!" Her arms were powdered with flour up to the elbows from preparing pies.

"What did you say?" Father asked Cam, pausing as they were about to pass.

"Oh . . . I . . ." stammered Cam, but just then Carlyle ran up the stairs behind him.

"Father," she cried, seeing her brother's predicament, "we've had ever so many adventures! And we went to see Mrs. Firstpenny, too!"

"I know," Father replied. "We phoned." He reached out and plucked a leaf from her hair.

"Where in the world is your hair ribbon?" Mother asked. "You and your brother look like two of Chief Temescal's warriors. Hurry and get cleaned up for dinner."

"Oh! Oh! Oh!" moaned the Hort in terror. "Two of them! Aren't you scared to death? Oh, those big, ugly things!"

Cam darted up the stairs and dashed into his room, Tee-Bo at his heels.

"That was close!" he gasped as he dropped his bundle on the bed, with a sigh of relief.

Carlyle rushed in a moment later. "What shall we do now?" she asked. "About the . . . you know?" She looked meaningfully at the Hort's legs, which were turning visible again. But the poor fellow saw them himself at the same time and set up such a howl that the two children were thrown into a panic. Cam had to threaten to muzzle him once more.

Carlyle cast a glance about her brother's room, which was warm and bright, with long streamers of the setting sun moving over the polished floor.

"It's too warm and dry in here. Horts have to keep moist."

"I'm cooking," Uncle Rotten Hort whimpered, looking fearfully down at his legs. "I'm cooking, and it's all your fault! I'd be better off muzzled to death than cooked into a brown roast, you ugly big things!"

Then he began to howl and shriek and blubber worse than before.

"For Pete's sake—" Cam started to shout, but Tee-Bo interrupted.

"Put him in the shower! Soak him good! Drown him, for all we care!"

Cam scooped up the Hort and dashed into the bathroom, Carlyle and Tee-Bo following.

"Hot or cold?" asked the boy, setting the Hort, not too gently, right in the center of the tub.

"Forevermore," Tee-Bo snapped, "cold, of course! You don't want to parboil him!"

Cam turned on the water, and a fine spray streamed out. The Hort ceased screaming instantly, with a gulp of surprise.

"Make it as fine as possible," Carlyle suggested, "then it will be something like it was in the cavern."

Uncle Rotten Hort looked at the three of them with a sly squint.

"This isn't . . . couldn't be . . . *muzzling*, now, could it?"

"Nope," replied Cam cheerfully. "Muzzling is too horrible to talk about."

The Hort frowned and then began to grin as the cool spray restored the silver transparency of his skin.

Nevertheless, he had to be tied to prevent his escape, and this was done with a couple of Carlyle's long stockings. The children apologized for the inconvenience but reminded him that it was his own fault.

"This is remarkable," said he with a nod of great satisfaction. "I didn't think thee had anything as clever as this. Is this a form of punishment to thee, then?"

Cam laughed. "Only to Tee-Bo." He ruffled the dog's fur as he spoke. "Your idea really saved the day, Tee-Bo, and just in the nick of time."

"Now, you behave yourself, Uncle Rotten Hort," Carlyle told him as they prepared to leave. "I'll bring you something for dinner as soon as I can."

At the dinner table, Mother told about Mrs. Firstpenny's discovery. After describing it, she said, "It doesn't sound like any egg I've ever heard of. Do you suppose it could really be a fossilized roc's egg? Or an *ostrich* egg?"

Father, who was eating dinner somewhat hastily so dessert would come sooner, could think only of the Elder-Whipple Pie quivering on the sideboard.

"Uh—where did you say she found this remarkable object?" he asked, but only out of politeness, since he was very keen on pie, as we know.

"In the hay in her barn. She went to gather eggs, and there it was."

Father settled back in his chair, ready for dessert.

"Maybe a fossilized roc walked in and laid it. As for an ostrich, it seems unlikely."

"You saw it, didn't you, children?" asked Mother.

"Yes," Carlyle answered, with a lump in her throat because she felt guilty. "It's pretty big."

"Don't mumble, child," Father said. "How big would you say it was, Carlyle?"

"About the size of a roc's egg," the little girl replied, rushing her words all together.

"Then it must *be* a roc's egg, and since we all agree on this, may we now have dessert?"

The Elder-Whipple Pie was a supreme success. It was made of nectarines, crabapples, and whipped cream, the combination Father liked best. When the dinner things were cleared away, Mother and Father walked down the street to visit the Flannellas, and the children began an immediate plan of attack for rescuing the Great Wet-Stone.

"Did you see Mother's face when she was talking about Mrs. Firstpenny?" asked Carlyle. "She knows how much this means to her. Mrs. Firstpenny hasn't *ever* in her whole life *ever* found anything like this before."

"Neither has anyone else, Carly," remarked Cam.

Tee-Bo cast an anxious glance at the ceiling. "The tub won't overflow, will it?"

"I left the drain open," Cam said, "and the spray's so light no one can hear it."

"What shall we take him to eat?" Carlyle asked. "It has to be wet and cold like their fern cakes and trillium tea."

They decided on a small slice of pie and a glass of iced tea, and, remembering the elegant manner in which they had been served by the Horts, they used Mother's best china and finest glassware.

Uncle Rotten Hort was curled up in the tub, dozing under the cool spray. At first he eyed the food suspiciously, but, as Father had so often said, no one could resist Mother's pie, and after one taste, he gobbled it up, smacking his lips in pleasure.

"Thee must give the recipe to Gracious Hort to turn over to the Royal Kitchens," he declared, forgetting that he was their deadly enemy and had brought them great trouble.

"Do you think he's sorry he's been so wicked?" Carlyle asked when they were back in Cam's room, with the door shut. "He keeps saying 'thee' all the time."

"Sorry or not, it's too late," Cam said sourly. "The damage is done, and if we don't get the Wet-Stone back to the Horts by tomorrow, you know what will happen!"

"Think of how sad they must be tonight." Carlyle's

eyes filled with tears of sympathy.

Tee-Bo leaped up onto the bed beside her. "It's not as bad as it was, Carly. At least, we know where the Wet-Stone *is*."

"It might as well be in Kokonor," Cam decided gloomily. "Mrs. Firstpenny will *never* give it up!"

12
An Extraordinary Plan, If It Works!

Cam began to pace the floor, a worried frown wrinkling his forehead. Now that they knew where the Great Wet-Stone was, they were worse off than before. The room was so quiet that they could hear the clock ticking over the soft hiss of the shower. Carlyle sniffed once or twice and sighed heavily.

Abruptly Tee-Bo stood up on the bed and shook himself. He stared at the children through shaggy bangs.

"What if it really did . . . *hatch?*" he asked, in a curious tone.

"Don't be funny," Cam said.

123

"I'm not trying to be funny, boy," the dog replied in the same serious vein. "I merely asked, 'What if it'—"

"Hatched," Cam finished, "which is ridiculous. It isn't an egg, you know."

"It just looks like an egg," Carlyle said, patting Tee-Bo.

"I know it isn't an egg," the dog went on. "I wasn't born yesterday, you know, but no one seems to want to answer my question: What if it *hatched?*"

"Botheration—" Cam began impatiently, but the dog held up a restraining paw.

"Calm down a moment, boy," he requested, "and let me explain."

"You have a plan, haven't you?" Carlyle asked, her face brightening.

The dog nodded. "I might have. First, an answer to my question: What if this wonderful 'egg' that your friend has should *hatch?* Why, then, she wouldn't have an egg anymore, would she?"

"She hasn't got an egg now," Cam put in crossly. "She's got the Horts' Great Wet-Stone."

"Ah, but she doesn't know it, now, does she?" cried Tee-Bo triumphantly. "She thinks it's an egg, and eggs do hatch, now, don't they?"

Cam stopped pacing and came slowly back to the bed, where he sat down and stared at the dog.

"But if something hatches," he said slowly, not understanding yet, "something has to come out of the egg—I mean, out of the Great Wet-Stone."

"*Exactly*," cried Tee-Bo, bouncing on the bed with excitement, "and that's my plan!"

"You mean we have to put something there," the boy queried, "to make Mrs. Firstpenny think it *hatched?*"

"Right! And *we* take the Great Wet-Stone!"

The children regarded him in astonishment. "B-But," Carlyle asked, "won't Mrs. Firstpenny be disappointed?"

"Not if it's big enough and grand enough," the dog declared. "She'll be prouder than ever. You'll see!"

"Something bigger and better than the Horts' Great Wet-Stone," Cam said slowly, "would have to be really something. It won't work, Tee-Bo."

"We can't break Mrs. Firstpenny's heart," Carlyle agreed sadly.

"Come, now," the dog said, "we've gone this far; let's not give up."

"It would have to be an elephant or an ostrich," Cam sighed, "or a goose that lays golden eggs. Sorry, Tee-Bo, but your solution isn't very practical."

"Wait a minute," interrupted Carlyle, a strange expression on her face. "It's a very practical solution, and so is yours, Cam. Why *not* a goose? Just a plain goose—not one that lays golden eggs, naturally. We could leave a goose in place of the Great Wet-Stone, and Mrs. Firstpenny would never suspect a thing!"

"How about the poultry commissioner? He's coming tomorrow," Cam reminded her.

"He's never seen the Wet-Stone," Carlyle said. "He'll only see the goose."

"How will we get a goose?" Cam asked.

"Easy. There's a goose farm at Elbow's Bend."

"Order it!" Tee-Bo suggested, his chin whiskers dancing in excitement.

"Order it?"

"Like Mother does from the store."

"We'll need money."

They went in search of all the money they could find, looking through their pockets and dresser drawers, and could only come up with one dollar, until Carlyle remembered four crisp dollar bills that Aunty Hi had sent her for a birthday present.

"Is five dollars enough for a goose?" she asked, wondering what she had been going to buy and suddenly remembering that she had been saving for a new diary.

"It had better be," Cam said grimly, "or ours is cooked!"

"Just having heard the worst pun of the year," announced Tee-Bo, "I'm going to retire. We have a hard day ahead of us, and we're not out of the woods yet!"

"We're not even *in* the woods yet!" retorted Cam, and immediately the two children and the dog had a short pillow fight and a free-for-all, just because they felt so much better. If their plan worked, they could still save the Horts.

When Carlyle awoke the next morning, the sun was pouring through the window and Mother was smiling at her.

"Wake up, sleepyhead! One of you left the shower on all night! I just turned it off."

"Oh, poor Uncle Rotten Hort!" cried the little girl, jumping out of bed and running down the hall to the bathroom.

"I beg your pardon?" said Mother, staring after her.

"I have to tell Cam," she flung over her shoulder.

"He knows. I already told him," Mother replied.

"Cam! Wake up!" Carlyle shook him vigorously. "Mother turned off the water!"

At this, Cam, who had gone back to sleep, opened his eyes, leaped out of bed, and rushed into the bathroom.

"He's gone!" he whispered, staring frantically around the room.

Mother's voice floated up the stairs. "Breakfast in ten minutes!"

"Where could he have gone?" Carlyle was staring into the empty tub.

Cam slapped his hand against his pajama pocket.

"That's it!" he cried. "We don't have our lapis lazuli!"

He ran into his bedroom, returning a moment later with the stone. There was the Hort, peacefully sleeping, as though he hadn't a care in the world. His hair was damp; his clothes were damp; and he was as silvery as ever.

"He's there!" he whispered, tiptoeing out. "He's asleep."

"I'm going right over to Idora's," Mother was saying as the children came downstairs, ready for breakfast, "to see her wonderful egg."

Father looked at her doubtfully. "Have you forgotten the date?"

"Oh-oh!" Mother's eyes flew back from the calendar. "Correction. We're going to the lecture first."

"And I think the children should go, too. They're quite old enough," Father added.

Mother, going from the stove to the table, paused to press the tip of her nose against the screen door.

"Nothing can match a late summer day," she commented, staring over the glistening lawn. "Every

leaf and bug is absolutely mad with joy." She sat at the table and took up her fork. "There won't be many more days like this."

"Fresh air is good for children," Cam remarked, sipping his orange juice slowly.

"And children need to walk and run a lot, too," Carlyle said thoughtfully. "It makes them big and strong."

Father looked speculatively from one to the other.

"I'm getting the impression that I'm an unpopular minority at the moment. Now, would anyone care to elaborate?"

"Well"—Mother filled his cup—"you see, it's the last day of summer vacation. They'll be at books and lectures soon enough." She watched Father's expression. "We could put it to a vote."

"Oh, certainly!" Father cleared his throat and assumed his most professorish air. "Those preferring to ride in Old Bessie through the heat and dust to the crowded, noisy city and those who want to be penned up in an auditorium full of bores, raise their hands." There was a fraction of a pause. "No hands," remarked Father, pretending to be amazed. "Very well. Now, those preferring to romp and run barefoot through the woods with their dog, raise— Wait! Wait! Not your voices; your hands!" They were already cheering him.

"Now you will have strong and healthy children," Mother said, after she had kissed him and rumpled his hair.

"What about you?" asked Father. "You didn't raise your hand either time."

"I don't need fresh air and sunshine. I'm already strong and healthy, and I adore lectures—with you."

Before Mother left, she reminded the children that she would be home at four and that she wanted to find them there waiting for her.

"Then we can go to Mrs. Firstpenny's together," she concluded.

"That was a close call!" Tee-Bo said, coming in as Mother and Father departed. "What would we have done if Father had made you go to that lecture?"

"Fainted dead away," sighed Carlyle. "Life's complicated enough as it is."

"Life is simple," corrected her brother. "We're what's complicated. Carly, get the phone book. It's time to get started."

13
MacCorkle Delivers the Goods

"The very first thing we have to do," Cam went on, "is to get the phone book and look up the number of the goose farm."

"I'll get it," Carlyle said. She returned a moment later with the book. "I don't know the name of the place. I just know it's a goose farm."

"Try the Yellow Pages," Tee-Bo urged.

"At least we know it's in Elbow's Bend."

Carlyle flipped the pages. "Goose is poultry, isn't it?"

"Forevermore," Tee-Bo exclaimed, "we forgot about the poultry commissioner!"

"That's right!" Carlyle's face showed her dismay. "He's going to Mrs. Firstpenny's to see the egg—I mean, the Great Wet-Stone!"

"That's what I'm saying," the dog interjected, "so why don't you phone him, Cam, and tell him not to come until tomorrow?"

"For Pete's sake!" Cam shook his head indignantly. "I'm not a lady!"

"But you can imitate Mrs. Firstpenny's voice," his sister said. "That's what Tee-Bo means. I'll look up that number first."

They couldn't find a number for the poultry commissioner and wasted a lot of valuable time searching for it, until Carlyle thought of asking Information, who kindly explained about such things and gave them the number.

"It's 'City and County Offices,'" Cam said gloomily, for he was doing the phoning, "and that operator thinks I have bats in my belfry."

"Did she *say* so?" asked Tee-Bo, with an incredulous look.

"Ssh!" said Carlyle as her brother began dialing the number.

They waited, listening to the phone ring on the other end.

"Hello?" Cam said suddenly, his voice high and thin, sounding so much like Mrs. Firstpenny that

Carlyle clapped her hands over her mouth to stifle a giggle.

"Good morning! This is Mrs. Idora Firstpenny, in Riverview," said Cam, his face turning pink. "Yes, I would like to speak to the poultry commissioner, please. . . . Yes. . . . Who? *Who?* . . . Oh, I guess so. . . . Yes. Mr. Turkletop, if that's his name— Carly, will you stop!" Cam suddenly roared, in his own voice, and then changed quickly back to the old lady's. "Yes, I will. Thank you very much."

He hung up and faced the other two. "He's left already. He had an appointment at Tackatoo, but he'll be at Mrs. Firstpenny's by one o'clock. She told me so. She thought I was Mrs. Firstpenny."

"You sounded just exactly like her!" Carlyle snickered. "I'm sorry I laughed."

"That means we have to get there before he does," Tee-Bo groaned. "What did you say the commissioner's name is?"

"Turkletop," Cam told him. "Why does he have to go so early?"

Carlyle had her nose close to the Yellow Pages.

"I found it!" she said, looking up. "It's Mac-Corkle's Poultry Farm, number three ShyAnne Road, Elbow's Bend!"

She read the number to Cam.

"Who do I talk like now?" he asked.

"Father!" Tee-Bo responded promptly. "Be masterful! Don't let them put you off!"

"Right!" Carlyle added, a note of desperation in her voice. "This is our last chance to save the Horts!"

"Well, don't expect a miracle," her brother grumbled. He dialed, and once more they could hear the phone ringing at the other end. Someone said, "Hello," so loudly that the boy jumped. Then he raised his head with a jaunty air and said, "Hello. Is this MacCorkle's Poultry Farm?" He sounded as if he was enjoying his new role, for he had made his voice low and deep and friendly, like Father's.

"What?" he said, and then again, "What?" with a terrible scowl. He put down the receiver and stared at his sister. "Rose's Glue Shop!"

Carlyle looked again. "I'm sorry. I had my finger on the wrong one."

Cam dialed the correct number, and the other two listened while he ordered a goose to be delivered to their address as soon as possible.

"Yes, number thirty-seven Selah Road, Riverview. . . . Yes, I'd be glad to: S-e-l-a-h, Selah Road, Riverview. . . . An *old* goose, you say? . . . Still able to walk? . . . Well, I think this will not matter too much, young man. . . . Oh, I see! . . . Yes. . . . Yes. . . . Thank you very much indeed!"

He turned from the phone, grinning widely.

"They're bringing it in about forty-five minutes!"

"An *old* goose?" Carlyle asked, frowning. "How can an *old* goose come out of an egg?"

"Forevermore!" Tee-Bo's chin whiskers were quivering in sudden agitation. "We forgot something else! When things hatch, aren't there usually some messy bits of eggshell lying about? How'll we manage that?"

Cam looked startled for a moment, then smiled confidently. "If *you* found a big goose where a big egg had been," he asked Tee-Bo, "would *you* be thinking about eggshells?"

Tee-Bo, briefly considering that unlikely situation, shook his head. "Not if I were Mrs. Firstpenny—I guess."

Cam nodded. "Now, we only have five dollars," he said, getting back to the immediate problem. "What if that isn't enough?"

"You can charge it," Tee-Bo concluded. "There's too much at stake to quibble at this point."

"But an *old* goose," Carlyle persisted, her mouth drooping at the corners. "Wouldn't Mrs. Firstpenny like a young one better?"

"We have to take what we can get," Cam told her firmly. "Carly, get the money. Now, how are we going to carry a goose all the way out to Mrs. Firstpenny's?"

"Can't it walk?"

"I thought geese could fly."

"But we have to hide it. We don't want anybody to see it!"

"Take your red wagon."

"And what about Uncle Rotten Hort?"

For several minutes, words flew about the room in a whirlwind as they made plans, unmade them, and then thought up new ones.

Half an hour went by. Carlyle took iced tea and pie to the Hort and explained that they would soon be taking him back to the forest.

"I rather like it here," the old fellow protested. "Don't forget to give me the recipe for this—what do you call it?"

"Elder-Whipple," the little girl replied. "It's pie."

She ran downstairs and found the others staring out the window.

"No one yet," Tee-Bo said glumly.

A half hour passed. By now it was ten o'clock, and Cameron was scowling and fidgeting.

"Maybe he had a flat tire," Tee-Bo sighed.

"Or lost the address," added Carly.

"Or the goose."

The minutes ticked by. Carlyle tried to read a book but kept losing the place, because her eyes were always going to the window from which any car that drove up would be plainly visible. Cam cartwheeled about the room, until the dog requested politely that he stop because he was making him nervous.

The clock struck eleven.

Tee-Bo could not sit still. "I'll just run down the street. I'm bound to see if he's coming."

At eleven thirty, no one had arrived, and Tee-Bo had run up and down the block fourteen times.

"I'm a nervous wreck," he panted, his chin whiskers quivering. "I'll probably fall into a dead faint if he *does* get here!"

Carlyle mopped his forehead with a damp towel and filled his bowl with cool water.

"Go jump in the tub with Uncle Rotten Hort," Cam grumbled. "That'll cool you off!" This resulted in Carlyle's declaring Cam was just plain rude, Tee-Bo's sniffing and saying that one must consider the source, and Cam's instantly apologizing and admitting that he couldn't stand the suspense, either.

At eleven forty-five, a truck was heard driving up their street. It stopped in front of the house. It had slats for sides, and on it was painted MacCorkle's Poultry Farm.

"He's here!" Carlyle whispered, turning pale. "Tee-Bo, don't you dare faint!" She was trembling all over.

"Get away from the window!" hissed Cam. "If you're nervous, wait in the kitchen. I'll handle this."

The doorbell rang and Cam answered. There stood a man in white overalls, a piece of torn paper in his hand.

"Dr. McRae's residence?" the man asked. His voice was patient and tired, his face red with the heat.

"Oh, yes," Cam replied. "Have you brought our goose?"

The man jerked his head. "In the truck. I know I'm late. Thought your father said 'Salad Road' and I been all over kingdom come."

"Would you like a cold drink?" asked the boy.

"No, thanks a lot, kid. I gotta get back. Have your father sign this, while I get it outta the truck."

Carlyle came to the door. "Is it a *very* old goose?"

"Well, she's no spring chicken!" the man chuckled. "Where ya want it? In the garage?"

"In the backyard, please," Cam requested. "I'll hold the gate for you. Oh, by the way, how much do we owe you?"

The man said he would have to look at the bill and went back to the truck, while the children raced to the backyard.

"Have you got the money, Carly?"

She held up the envelope. "Four one-dollar bills, six dimes, seven nickels, and five pennies. Exactly five dollars."

"I hope it's enough," Cam muttered grimly.

They held the back gate open while the man in white overalls carried in a crate so large that it all but hid him from view. Inside was an enormous mass of whitish gray feathers, with nothing else visible.

"Doesn't it have a head?" Tee-Bo whispered, keeping his distance.

"Is it really a *very* old goose, Mr. MacCorkle?" asked Carlyle.

The man smiled. "I'm Dan, not MacCorkle. Sure, she's old, but she's all we had." He looked at Cam. "Your father home, son?"

"No," Cam replied, adding quickly, "How much is the bill?"

The man handed him a slip of paper. "Five forty-five. Sign here."

"Five dollars and forty-five cents!" Carlyle cried, staring as if she were hypnotized.

"That does it!" Tee-Bo cried and ran under the bench in a state of collapse.

Cam signed and handed back the pen. Then he looked him straight in the eye.

"My father has commissioned me to tell you, in his absence, that he only has five dollars."

There was a short silence while the driver stared at Cam, then at the house and grounds, and finally back at the boy.

"Uh-huh," he sighed.

"Here it is, Mr. MacCorkle," Carlyle said, "in this envelope. We can mail the forty-five cents to you in about two weeks, Father said."

"Gulp!" came from Tee-Bo under the bench.

The driver took the envelope and counted the money carefully. Then he scratched his head, looked around once more, and nodded. "Okay, kids. Tell your father to send it in two weeks—if he can spare it."

The children thanked him and watched him drive away.

"Quick!" cried Cam. "Bring the wagon! I'll get a hammer!"

14
A Most Cooperative Goose

There was a bustle of activity for a moment or two, and then the three conspirators gathered beside the crate.

"It must be very old," Carlyle sighed, peering through the slats at the mound of feathers.

"I hope it's alive," Tee-Bo muttered, squinting through his bangs.

Cameron knelt and began to pry open a slat. "If we expect to get there before the poultry commissioner," he grunted, his face red with exertion, "we're going to have to hustle. Bring the wagon and something to cover the goose with, so no one can see it." He poked the feathers gingerly with one finger. "Is it asleep?"

"I hope so," Tee-Bo said fervently. "If it isn't, it's dead!"

When Carlyle returned with the wagon and a blanket, her brother had all the slats off one side and was timidly attempting to coax the goose out of the crate.

"Pull it," Carlyle suggested, after watching and seeing nothing happening.

"Pull *what?*" the boy asked, since nothing was visible but feathers.

"Its leg—or something."

"I'm not sure it has any."

"Cam, it's twelve thirty already!"

"For Pete's sake . . ." he muttered and then reached into the mass of feathers and began groping. Suddenly there was a trembling and allover quivering of the feathers, and a sound like steam hissing from a kettle issued forth. The boy jumped back, and the mound of feathers quieted down.

The three looked at one another.

"I don't know much about geese," Cam admitted.

Carly turned to Tee-Bo. "*You* talk to it."

"Me?" sputtered Tee-Bo. "Why me? I don't know what to say to a goose!"

"That's ridiculous," Carlyle said. "Just explain where we're going and why."

"And ask it to cooperate," Cam added.

"Oh, forevermore!" exclaimed the dog, backing away gingerly and then returning, with a resigned look.

"You'd better!" Cam said grimly.

Tee-Bo sank down on his haunches by the half-open crate. "Goose," he began, "we have to take you to Mrs. Firstpenny's farm, and we have to get there before the poultry commissioner does." He paused. Still there was no sign of life within the crate. "What now?" he asked.

"Tell it how nice it is at Mrs. Firstpenny's and how kindhearted she is," Carlyle replied hurriedly. "We don't have time to explain about the Horts."

Tee-Bo dutifully repeated what he had been told to and was describing the farm and how clean and pretty it was, when suddenly the whole mass of feathers came to life and a neck rose up like a periscope. It was topped by a flat head, from which glittered two alert eyes. Making a faint hissing sound, the goose stepped from the crate and began strutting awkwardly about, as though needing to stretch its legs.

Surprisingly enough, the dog neither drew back nor showed any degree of apprehension.

"She says she was napping and didn't intend to be rude," he explained, regarding the goose with great curiosity. "Her name is Ethel, and she can't bear to be referred to as 'it.' This offends her."

"Ethel?" Carlyle asked. "Who named her Ethel?"

"Her parents, naturally," replied the dog, who was very quick at getting answers from the goose, though the others couldn't understand a word.

"Ask her to get in the wagon—quick," Cam said. "I suppose it—I mean, she—won't like an old hot blanket over her, will she?"

"I'm explaining that she has to travel incognito for a while," Tee-Bo told them. A strange expression then crossed his face, and he turned his head aside. "She thinks it's *cute!*" he whispered hoarsely.

To their delight, the old goose waddled over to the wagon and settled herself in it as though it were the royal carriage and she the queen—though somewhat awkwardly.

"She says she's not as young as she used to be," the dog explained, still whispering.

Carlyle spread the blanket carefully. "I'm sorry I have to do this, Ethel," she apologized. "We'll take it off the minute we're in the woods."

They started out of the yard, Cam pulling the wagon and the blanket concealing the uneven lump beneath it.

"What about Uncle Rotten Hort?" Cam asked as they advanced up the sidewalk.

"He'll be all right," Carlyle said. "I left the shower on."

"I hope we're not too late!" Tee-Bo murmured, bounding alongside and carefully tending the blanket to see that it didn't drag.

The street was still and deserted. Everyone was in town buying school supplies. The summer sun beat down, and Cam's face grew redder as he pulled faster, with Carlyle pushing from behind.

"You'll have to excuse the bumps and everything, Ethel," she panted, "but we have to hurry."

"She's fine," Tee-Bo informed her. "Just a little thirsty, she says."

When they crossed the bridge and arrived at the path that led to Mrs. Firstpenny's house, Cam pulled the wagon behind some bushes and told Carlyle to remove the blanket.

"She must be cooked by now."

But the goose appeared to be undamaged, and as soon as her feet touched the cool earth, she began hunting for bugs among the leaves.

"We'll take the shortcut through the woods," Cam announced. "Tee-Bo, make sure Ethel follows us and doesn't get lost."

"Righto!" Tee-Bo sang out, with the first muster of spirit he'd shown all day. Things were already looking better.

They were moving on through the woods, when Carlyle stopped short.

"Look!" she cried, pointing to the road they had just left. "There's a car!"

A fine big truck was driving slowly along the road toward them. The driver's head was poked far out the window as he peered anxiously in all directions.

"Keep Ethel in the bushes, out of sight," Cam called to Tee-Bo, while he and Carlyle watched the truck. It gleamed with fresh black and white paint and glittered with chrome.

"I guess it's just about one o'clock—or a little after," Carlyle whispered anxiously.

"It's probably the poultry commissioner, all right," Cam said with great finality. "Let's wait and see."

"Shouldn't we *hurry?*" she asked.

"It's too late. Besides, he's going to stop."

The driver, having spotted the children standing by the side of the road, drew carefully alongside and stopped the truck.

"You kids know where Old Farrow Road is?" He was holding a slip of paper in his hand, and, beneath the wide-brimmed rancher's hat, his face was red and perspiring. In fancy silver lettering on the door were the words *Poultry Commissioner*.

Carlyle pressed her lips tightly together, so she wouldn't say something she shouldn't, while her brother repeated after the man, "Old Farrow Road?" It was as if it were the first time he'd ever heard the name, though both children knew well that Mrs. Firstpenny lived there. It was such an old road and so well known that it didn't even have a sign on it.

"Old Farrow Road?" Cam repeated again, half closing his eyes and squinting at the man.

"Yeah. Number twenty-one. I. L. F. Firstpenny— or maybe Firstparty. They told me at the gas station to follow this road, but there aren't any signs."

"Well—" Cam stepped nearer to the truck, with a wiggle of his shoulders that his sister knew meant he was about to do something he disliked and would rather not do but had to. "Well—there aren't any signs, because everybody knows Old Farrow Road so well they don't need any."

"Yeah?" The driver scowled and stared down the road toward Mrs. Firstpenny's house, which, of course, was some distance away and well concealed by the woods. "This it?" he asked.

Cam swallowed and lifted his head masterfully. "You go along this road, all right, but you have to go back the other way." He pointed in the direction from which the truck had just come.

"Back that way?" The man's tone was unbelieving.

"If you want Old Farrow Road. You see"—Cam's voice became lower and more authoritative—"you have to go back the way you came, to that big building where the smokestack is. See it?"

The man shaded his eyes. "Why back there?"

"Because," Cam continued briskly, "that's the only way to get to Old Farrow Road. As soon as you reach the building with the smokestack, you turn right. That's Hollow Hill Lane."

"Turn right at Hollow Hill Lane," muttered the driver.

Cam nodded. "Hollow Hill Lane is really Old Farrow Road. Nobody ever got around to changing it. Follow Hollow Hill for about twenty minutes—"

"Twenty minutes?" the man exploded. "Twenty minutes!"

"It's an old road and unpaved," the boy explained patiently, "and you'll think there's nothing there, but pretty soon you'll see some trees and old houses. You can't miss them."

"Y' sure?"

"I've lived here all my life," Cam stated with simple dignity. "I know every road in Riverview. You can't miss it."

"Well, thanks," returned the driver. "Much obliged, kid." He looked up and down for a place to turn around and, finding none, began backing the truck down the road he had just traveled.

"Good luck!" called the boy. The driver waved, and

the children watched him turn around, driving the shining big black and white truck off in the direction of the building with the smokestack.

"Oh, dear!" said Carlyle as her brother turned around to join her.

"I know," he answered crossly. "I told a lie, and I feel terrible."

"He was so nice."

"I had to." Cam's face was miserable but determined. "For the Horts."

Carlyle sighed. "I know it. Let's hurry!"

Together they ran back to the pathway, where Tee-Bo was waiting with Ethel.

"Was it old Turkletop?" cried Tee-Bo as soon as he saw them. Ethel was scooping up bugs at a fierce pace, as though she'd never seen one before.

"Yes, it was." Cam spoke shortly.

"Tell Ethel we have to hurry," Carlyle urged. "Make her stay on the path."

"Right!" said the dog smartly, running up to the goose, who, in turn, obligingly waddled along as nimbly as she could, the children following.

"Is he going to Mrs. Firstpenny's?" Tee-Bo panted.

Carlyle shook her head. "Not for a long while. Cam sent him to Hollow Hill Lane. He said it was really Old Farrow Road and that he had to drive on it for about twenty minutes before he would find number twenty-one." She sighed. "He was nice, and Cam hated to do it."

"Forevermore!" The dog's eyes rolled. "He may spend some time up in the old quarry before he finds his way back!"

"That's what we're counting on," Cam said crossly, "so let's hurry and get this thing over with! Can't you make Ethel go any faster?"

Tee-Bo looked apologetic. "She's never been near a forest before in her whole life. She can't believe it!" He paused, turning his head in embarrassment. "She said it's goose heaven, and we're—angels!"

"Wow," said Cam.

"If she likes it here," Carlyle declared, "she'll love it at Mrs. Firstpenny's."

To do Ethel justice, she *was* trying to hurry. So many new and strange bugs and plants and smells attracted her that she would stop and then dart off the path after a particularly tantalizing something and forget what she was supposed to do, until Tee-Bo had to remind her, and then she would waddle on once more.

But when they reached Farrow's Pond, lying like a dark sheet of glass beneath the trees, disaster struck and almost put an end to all their plans.

15
The Incantation

Ethel, when she first saw the glint of the water, stopped short. Then, with a wild hiss, she flapped her wings and, without so much as a by-your-leave, swept low over the ground and landed with a great splash—*kerplunk!*—right in the middle of the pond.

If the children thought this was just an interlude and she would get out soon and resume her hurried pace, they were mistaken. She apparently went temporarily berserk with joy. First she skimmed over the water; then she dove and disappeared, surfacing several yards distant and skating madly off over the top of the water as though she had just that moment been given the leading role in the *Swan Lake* ballet and was late for rehearsal. Then she spun around in the water, then skimmed, then dove, then skated, then spun again—until the others grew dizzy watching her.

Cam called and threatened; Tee-Bo called and threatened; Carlyle called and begged; but Ethel, in a transport of delight, turned a deaf ear.

Cam's face was dark with despair. "This could go on for several years."

"Sorry." Tee-Bo felt that he was somehow to blame. "All that water's really gone to her head, I guess."

"Oh, dear!" Carlyle almost wept. "Just when everything was going right!"

At this, a rusty old voice spoke up, almost in their ears. "What in thunderation is going on here?"

The children jumped and looked around. "Matchlock!" they cried, spying the huge old toad, his shoulders half out of the water, regarding them from the edge of the pond.

"What in thunderation is *that*, and what's it doing in my pond?"

"Oh, Mr. Matchlock," Carlyle cried, "it's a goose, and if we don't get her out of here and take her to Mrs. Firstpenny's right away, we'll never get the Great Wet-Stone back to the Horts!"

"Oho!" Matchlock rumbled deep in his throat. "So you found it!"

The three then proceeded to relate, very briefly, the events leading up to their dilemma. The old toad nodded and blinked as he listened, water dimpling and running down his back and sides. When they had finished, he stared impatiently at Carlyle.

"Why don't you cast a spell on the old thing? I'll hide deep down in the mud so I won't be hurt, and you say an incantation—a horrible, shivery, searing, blasting, crashing, and exquisite one!"

The children were silent.

"Why not?" demanded their friend eagerly, beginning to shiver in an agony of delight. "Oh, do it! Do it! Do it! I pray, do it!"

"Well—" the little girl began, looking sideways at her brother. "Well—"

"My sister's incantations," spoke up Cam, coming neatly to the rescue, "are so powerful, you see, that they can be used only at special times. Otherwise"— he snapped his fingers—"disaster!"

Matchlock, on hearing this, fell to shivering so violently that water flew off him in all directions. "I know it! I know it!" he roared. "Disaster! Incredibly gorgeous and preposterously magnificent disaster! Oh, do it! Do it! Do it!"

"She can't," Cam stated. "She can't do it now."

The old toad instantly grew still. He even came a few inches farther out of the water.

"Why not, pray?"

"She can't do it now, because last night was the full of the moon!"

Matchlock nodded. "So it was. So it was."

"She can't work a spell until two days after the full of the moon, unless—" Here Cam stopped and held up one hand, as though making a magic sign.

"Unless what?" Matchlock begged, his eyes bulging more than ever.

"Unless you help her. Then she can do it, and it will work."

"Even if last night was"—here the old fellow dropped his voice to a thundering whisper—"*the full of the moon?*"

Cam nodded.

"What do I do, boy? What does old Matchlock have to do? Tell me! Tell me!"

Cam stared out over the waters of Farrow's Pond. Ethel was skimming along at a great pace, observing her own gliding shadow beneath her, apparently unaware of the giant toad half-submerged at the children's feet.

"While my sister stands here," Cam told him, taking a few steps and drawing a circle with one finger in the damp sand, "and says the incantation, you must leap into the air three times and roar out with all your might each time."

Matchlock stared in surprise. "That'll make a mighty big splash," he said finally, "and, besides, what if I get some of the spell on me? What will happen to me?"

"That's ridiculous," Cam said impatiently. "My sister's been casting spells for years. She knows what she's doing."

"I should think," Tee-Bo said pointedly, "that you would trust the talents of anyone clever enough to find the Horts' Wet-Stone and thereby save the whole country of the Horts."

"You've done that, now?" Matchlock replied, weighing the matter.

"It's just about done," Cam assured him, "but we do need your help right now."

"What a day!" bubbled the old fellow, who seemed lost in contemplation of his own good fortune. "A real, live incantation, and old Matchlock gets to help! All right," he went on, "I'll do it! You're quite positive I'm not in the spell?"

"Quite positive," Carlyle assured him, moving into the exact center of the circle Cam had drawn.

"You're fortunate," the boy said, regarding the toad with a mysterious air, "to be able to witness a genuine spell during the full of the moon. This will be something to tell your friends."

"To be sure," agreed Matchlock, nervously watching Carlyle, "but I can't bear it, you know! I may swoon! But do it! Do it! Do it!"

Carlyle shut her eyes and drew a deep breath. Then she crossed her arms and grasped her earlobes with her fingers. While the others waited in tense silence, she began, in low and solemn tones:

> *"Aus, ausser, bei, mit,*
> *Nach, siet,*
> *Von*
> *Zu!"*

She had barely reached *Zu!* when Matchlock, who had been quivering like a great bowl of jelly, took off with a roar that shook the trees. He came down, with a monstrous splash, in the middle of Farrow's Pond, with the water frothing and churning about him and the birds fluttering away with shrill cries of alarm.

Ethel, who had been doing circles—and very neat ones, too—had just cast a quick look over her shoulder, to make sure her audience was watching, and, of course, got an unobstructed view of the giant toad as he lunged into the air. With a shriek that could have been heard as far away as Elbow's Bend, the old goose shot straight up into the air and, without a backward glance, sailed over the treetops and dropped out of sight.

"She's out!" Cam yelled, and he began running after her as fast as he could, Tee-Bo following.

"Mr. Matchlock," called Carlyle as the toad came dripping and bubbling out of the water, "I have to go now, but I'll be back."

"B-B-But," sputtered the toad, "I only jumped once! I was so scared, I thought I would jump out of my skin, I did! Oh, delicious, delightful, and incredible scariness! I could hardly bear it! Do it again! Do it! Do it! Do it!"

"Not now," she replied, turning to go. "Some other time."

"Promise?" asked Matchlock.

"Promise."

And so, leaving the old fellow shaking happily at the thought of the awful incantations he would hear again, Carlyle ran through the forest after the others.

16
The Great Exchange

When Carlyle at last caught up with them, Cam was sitting on a stump, gloomily staring at the old goose, who rested on the ground, making faint hissing noises at Tee-Bo. Apparently they were conversing.

"Thank goodness you're here!" the dog exclaimed as she ran up. "Ethel was sure you'd been eaten by Matchlock."

"Now maybe we'll be able to get her to Mrs. First-penny's," Cam scolded as he stood up. "She wouldn't stir, not one step, without you."

"It's true," Tee-Bo nodded. "She's taken a great liking to you."

"I'm sorry you were frightened, Ethel," the little girl said, patting the creature's quivering feathers. "Matchlock's our friend, but, of course, you didn't know that."

Under the little girl's gentle touch, Ethel had risen and was now preening her feathers.

"She says you're very brave, and she wants to thank you for being her friend," Tee-Bo told her.

"I'll come to see her often," Carly replied, "when she lives with Mrs. Firstpenny."

The four of them hurried toward the old lady's house at the edge of the wood. As they approached it, Cam paused behind the shelter of trees.

"Here's our plan," he said, speaking rapidly and emphatically. "Tell Ethel that when I give the signal, she must follow me into the house. We'll go in the back way, while Carly keeps Mrs. Firstpenny out on the front porch, talking. Once Ethel's inside, she's got to stay there and behave herself, no matter what happens, until Mrs. Firstpenny finds her. Tell her, Tee-Bo, and hurry!"

The dog repeated all this to the goose, who bobbed her head understandingly.

"Be very quiet, Ethel," Carlyle added, "and don't frighten Mrs. Firstpenny. She's very timid as well as kindhearted."

Tee-Bo listened attentively to the goose's hissing

response. "She says she'll do exactly as you say, and please come to visit her often."

"I will. I promise." The little girl ran quickly out of the woods and across the garden to the front porch. To her surprise, the front door flew open before she could knock, and there stood Idora Firstpenny, nodding and beaming, wearing her best frilled apron.

"My!" cried the old lady, laughing happily. "I thought you were the poultry commissioner!"

"He isn't here yet, is he?" Carlyle stammered, before she could catch herself.

"I've been expecting him since one o'clock," was the answer, "and it's already past three. But I know he's a busy man. What a surprise I have for him!"

While she talked, her eyes scanned the road, up and down, but suddenly her glance dropped to the little girl before her.

"My soul, but you are hot and dusty, my dear! Do come in for a glass of lemonade and a bit of cold water on your face. I've a whole pitcherful ready for company, y'know."

Oh, dear, Carlyle thought miserably, *I hope she's as happy with Ethel as she is about the Horts' Great Wet-Stone! I hope we aren't doing something just terrible!* Aloud, she said, "Thank you, Mrs. Firstpenny," as the other paused on her way back into the house, "but I can't come in just now. I stopped by to . . . I stopped by to . . . ask if you had found any more giant eggs in your barn."

Out of the corner of her eye, she could see her brother stealthily leading Ethel toward the rear of the house, where they disappeared around the corner.

"Wasn't that something!" The old lady beamed, her face growing rounder and pinker with each word. "Imagine something like that in my barn! And I haven't a notion how long it had been there."

"How did you happen to find it?" Carlyle was straining her ears to catch the slightest noise within the house.

A dreamy look settled over Mrs. Firstpenny's face. "It gets lonely for an old lady by herself, very lonely indeed. Of course, I have old Heavingham, but he stays in the barn most of the time—though, I declare, I understand him as well as I do anybody; he's so bright, that dear fellow—but I can't very well have him into the parlor for tea. . . ."

Carlyle thought she heard something moving within, so she said quickly, in a rather loud voice, "Was it hidden in the hay or just lying there in plain sight?"

"Now, you know, that was strange," Mrs. Firstpenny answered. "It slips my mind just *why* I went to the barn that afternoon, but go I did. I figured I'd have a chat with dear old Heavingham before dinner. He'd been poorly for a day or so. . . ."

Now Carlyle distinctly heard something move in the house. "He's not sick, is he?" she shrieked and then clapped a hand over her mouth. If Ethel should hear and come out to find what was wrong, she felt she would die on the spot.

"My sakes, child! You startled me! Heavingham hasn't had a sick day in his life, but I thought I'd just cheer him up a mite, so I sat down in the old rocker by his stall, and I rocked and we chatted for a spell, and then a ray from the setting sun"—Carlyle saw Cam stealing slowly away from the house, casting furtive glances over one shoulder. He was alone— "came through the barn window," Mrs. Firstpenny said, "and I saw something glitter beneath the straw, and I got up and walked over to it—do you have to leave, child?—and there it was! I can't believe it to this hour! My dear, you're leaving?"

"I'm quite late," Carlyle assured her breathlessly, "but it's been interesting hearing about your discovery. Thank you very much."

"Come again," invited the old lady, smiling and nodding. "I'm expecting your mother later. We're to take tea together."

She was still standing there when Carlyle turned to wave from the edge of the woods, before racing off madly to find the others.

She hadn't taken ten steps before Tee-Bo bounded

up to her in a nervous frenzy of excitement.

"Forevermore," he shouted hoarsely, "hurry up! Cam's waiting by the falls!" He turned and ran.

"Has he got it?" she called, running after him. "Has he got the Great Wet-Stone?"

He called back something, but he was too far away for her to hear, so she ran toward the falls as fast as she could go, her heart pounding, expecting that at any moment Ethel would come screeching and hissing after her or even that Uncle Rotten Hort's face might peer at her from behind a tree.

When she reached the falls, so out of breath she couldn't say a word, the whole forest was still, as if every living creature knew exactly what was happening and waited in anxious anticipation. Cam was on the bank, and she knew from the way he stood, head up proudly and back very straight and military, that he'd been successful. Besides, his shirt bulged enormously in front, where he doubtless concealed the Great Wet-Stone. The moment he saw Carlyle, his face lit up, and he pointed to his shirtfront, a grin spreading from ear to ear.

"Won't the Horts be surprised!" he crowed. "I can't wait to see their faces when they see what we've got!"

Carlyle drew a deep breath. Now that the Horts seemed to be out of danger so soon, all her thoughts were with her friend Mrs. Firstpenny. Would she be

brokenhearted because the Wet-Stone was gone? Would she like Ethel? What if Ethel had misbehaved and frightened her?

"Oh, dear!" she exclaimed, looking miserable.

Cam scowled. "Now what?"

"I hope Ethel will be all right, and Mrs. Firstpenny, too. Oh, dear!"

"We can't worry about that," the boy declared. "We're going to see the Horts. Oh, what a grand surprise we have for them! Hurry up, Carly!"

He stepped jauntily out onto the first of the rocks that crossed the stream, his arms hugging his chest to protect the Great Wet-Stone. Then he stepped onto the next one, wobbling a bit because he could not extend his arms to maintain his balance.

"Watch out, boy!" Tee-Bo called in alarm as Cam slipped and then caught himself on the next step.

"What's the matter with you?" Carlyle called as she saw him still struggling to keep his balance.

"Get away! Stop it!" her brother said jerkily. He bent way back, as if trying to avoid something, and then straightened up, kicking furiously at the air with one foot. Then he moved violently forward, as if pushed from behind, and went ker*splash!* into the stream. He sat there, waist-deep in the cold water, with bubbles and ripples foaming and swishing around on all sides.

The other two watched in astonishment as he struggled to get to his feet and fell back into the water again.

"What's wrong?" Carlyle screamed again, losing her balance and almost following him into the stream as she tried to keep her eyes on him and on her own feet.

Tee-Bo was racing through the water, barking and growling and snapping at nothing, because he could see nothing to snap at.

Cam was still struggling, apparently fighting the water that surrounded him. "It's Wort Hort!" he shouted at the other two as he writhed and lunged in the stream, water flying in all directions. "It's Wort Hort, and he's trying to get the Wet-Stone! Shoo! Get away! Take that, Wort Hort! Take that!"

17
Cheers for Tee-Bo!

"We can't see anything!" screamed Carlyle in despair. "How can we help?"

Poor Cam was threshing about in the water frantically now, lunging out with both arms, now on his back, now on his face, gasping for breath as his head repeatedly went underwater. Tee-Bo dashed here and there, trying to find something to attack, while Carlyle shouted encouragement from the rock.

"Now there're two of them!" Cam cried suddenly, louder than ever. "Ouch! Get off me! Take that! Ouch, ouch!"

Though he fought desperately, it was plain that he

was losing the battle, and Carlyle was about to throw herself into the stream to help, when abruptly her brother sat upright, both arms clutching the precious Wet-Stone beneath his shirt, a look of amazement on his face.

"They've gone!"

"Where?" barked Tee-Bo, splashing madly about. "Where? Where?"

"How would I know? They're just gone!"

Cam stood up, drenched to the skin and dripping. "They might come back," he warned. "Let's get into the cave as fast as we can."

They scrambled over the rocks and through the dark entrance to the passageway. "Down the stairs, fast!" Cam took his sister's hand and pulled her after him.

They had barely reached the bottom of the moss-covered steps, when the great door to the Hort country began slowly to open, swinging wider and wider. The green light poured out and illuminated the pale, startled faces of the children. At the same time, loud cheers echoed throughout the vast, rocky chamber, and as the door opened wider, a huge company of Horts was revealed, standing there ready to greet them. They were dressed in festival robes and were clapping their hands rhythmically, meanwhile raising their thin little voices in cries of welcome. The entire kingdom must have been assembled, for as far as the children could see, there were throngs of Horts, their pale, silvery faces alight with joy and turned toward the new arrivals in happy expectation.

Courtly Hort stood before them all, a crown of blue stones resting on his head, and next to him, of course, good Gracious, clasping his arm and smiling proudly. Silken, more beautiful than ever in a gossamer gown of silver, stood by her mother.

The most astounding sight of all was Curly Hort. He was at one side, as though he had just entered the cavern. His one hand firmly clutched Uncle Rotten Hort himself, while his other gripped Wort Hort just as tightly. Neither Hort was struggling now, but both turned sullen and scowling faces on the group.

Courtly Hort stepped forward. "Welcome, good Cameron and good Carlyle! Thee have saved the entire kingdom of the Horts!"

He was so kingly that the children stared at him in awe, until Carlyle ran forward and took his hand. "Oh, Mr. Courtly Hort, you're really king again!"

"You're supposed to bow to a king," Tee-Bo said in a low voice, looking embarrassed.

"And don't call him 'Mister,'" Cam added. "He's a king now." The boy tried to bow but couldn't, because of the bulge beneath his shirt. "Your Majesty," he informed Courtly, "we've brought back the Great

Wet-Stone. It's under my shirt, but I'm afraid it's wet."

At this, the multitude broke into merry laughter, but King Courtly hushed them with an upraised hand and resumed speaking.

"We know thee have the Great Wet-Stone, good friend. May I say that this hour—an hour which was to have marked a deposed monarch's banishment into the Great Woods—has been transformed from one of tears and sorrow to one of great joy and prosperity." He paused while a ripple of pleasure traveled about the great hall. "And why? Solely because of the brave efforts of our three good heroes: good Cameron, good Carlyle, and good Tee-Bo!"

There were more cheers, whistles, and shouts at this, which echoed through the chamber until the king held up his hand for silence.

"Will the Royal Bearers step forth?"

Two stalwart Horts stepped up, bearing a jeweled platter between them.

"Now, Kluge, Brock, and Camel Hort, the Processional, if it please thee."

The three musicians, with delighted grins, raised their instruments and began the lively strains of a royal march. The king walked up to Cam and held out his hands, saying nothing. With an air of importance, Cam reached inside his shirt to remove the

Great Wet-Stone. The Wet-Stone was hard to remove because the cloth was soaking wet, but after a small struggle, it popped out, and, amid the gentle *ahs* and *ohs* of the Horts, the boy drew out the beautiful Stone and presented it to the waiting monarch. The music paused dramatically while Courtly Hort placed the Great Wet-Stone on the glittering surface of the jeweled platter. To the children's astonishment, it balanced itself perfectly, standing upright on its smaller end, while the Royal Bearers marched off with it and the music took up where it had left off. When the Stone had been placed solemnly in the Sacred Niche and its light was streaming steadily into the hall, the multitude broke into deafening cheers, the music went into a lively dance, and everyone's voice rose as one:

"Long live the king! Long live good King Courtly!"

When their voices had at last died away, the king called for the Royal Defenders. These were two official-appearing Horts, taller and more muscular than the others, who stepped up to relieve Curly Hort of his two prisoners.

"Uncle Rotten Hort," Carlyle called out, "how did you get out of our bathtub?"

The Hort turned a scowling face toward her. "That big, ugly giantess came upstairs to turn the water off and untied me, hee-hee, without even knowing I was there! Thee'll catch it, when thee gets home, for leaving the water on again!"

Cam stepped up and looked him straight in the eye. "My mother's not an ugly giantess, and you ought to be ashamed to talk like that!" He was turning aside to ask the king's pardon for speaking thus, when Uncle Rotten Hort interrupted, but in so altered a tone that everyone was shocked into silence.

"I know it," he said. "Thee are right. The giantess has a sweet face and manner, and her touch is as gentle as thistledown. When she unbound me, I felt the kindness in her very fingertips."

Wort Hort, who had done nothing but snivel and hurl malicious glances at everyone, now looked up into his uncle's face.

"Are we going to stop being wicked, Uncle?" he demanded peevishly.

The older Hort shrugged. "We have gained nothing and have lost much. Our deeds have caused only sorrow."

"Not to me!" Wort grumbled. "I was just getting good at it, too. Now I'll have to go back to singing, yah, yah, yah!" He began yelling hideously, until his uncle's threatening looks stopped him.

Gracious Hort had ordered an extra robe for Cam, who had been shivering in his wet clothes, but since the Horts' clothes were of gossamer, they did little to improve his condition, and now his teeth were chattering, and he was shaking with the cold.

Seeing this, the king made haste to wind up the immediate affair of the prisoners.

"If thee are repentant, good Rotten Hort," said he, "this bodes well. Punishment must be meted out, according to the law of our land, as soon as possible after the crime. So, as ruler of the Horts, I must pronounce sentence instantly."

At this, Wort Hort let out such a howl of anguish that Silken, leaving her place by Curly's side, rushed to him and threw her arms around him, bursting into tears.

"Thee must repent, too!" She wept. "Thee must repent, too!" She could say no more, for, although Wort Hort, who had been her friend and Curly's since childhood, had wounded her tender heart, she could not bear to see him suffer. Curly, after one startled look at his beloved, turned his face away, the glint of a tear in his eye, partly for Silken's grief and partly for the wickedness of a lifelong friend.

Wort Hort blushed scarlet with shame and then patted poor Silken on the shoulder. "Don't cry. Thee must not cry. I was really not *that* wicked." He looked at his uncle. "Shall I repent, too? I don't mind —much." Uncle Rotten Hort nodded, and Wort turned to Silken. "I repent, too, so stop bawling, please, dear Silken," he finished with a stammer.

While Silken took her place beside Curly, who was lending her his handkerchief for her tears, the king prepared to pronounce sentence.

18
The Sentencing

Everyone stood at strict attention, for there were rarely crimes in the country of the Horts, and this was the first one in the reign of their beloved King Courtly.

The king himself had turned slightly flushed, and everyone felt sorry for him. "Uncle Rotten Hort," he said solemnly, "choose a means by which thee will be able to serve our people, to make amends for the wrong thee has done, and if it please our sovereign will, it shall be granted."

The wicked Hort remained silent for a moment, his brows drawn. He knew the law of the land well and had been expecting just this. However, what evil schemes ran through his head no one was ever to know, for, to the surprise of all, his face creased in the first smile anyone had seen there for many a day.

"Your Majesty, since, according to law, I must be demoted from my former high rank, let me beseech thee to lower me to the Order of Grand Chef to your Majesty's table."

This was met by a murmur of astonishment from the crowd, and even the king appeared startled.

"Grand Chef," repeated Uncle Rotten Hort eagerly, "for I have lately learned of a recipe"—here he began smacking his lips—"a recipe for . . . for . . . oh, double drat, I've forgotten the name!"

"Elder-Whipple Pie," Carlyle said.

"Elder-Whipple Pie," went on the other swiftly, tossing the little girl an exasperated scowl, "a most elegant dish, which I hope to add to the Royal Cuisine. This is my request, O merciful king, and may I be known hereafter as Fat Hort, for that is what I shall no doubt become in my new capacity."

The Royal Scribe, who was taking all this down, now handed the written request to the king, who read it aloud and then asked for a vote. Of course, the Horts were by now very hungry, and the very mention of food brought unanimous consent. The former Uncle Rotten Hort, hence to be known as Fat Hort, must have taken all this into consideration, because ordinarily his punishment would have been far more severe. He might even have been demoted to the ignoble rank of Mixer of Trillium Tea and in such case would have been called Pour Hort, a name which, for some reason or other, was always the butt of many sly jokes and laughter on the part of the Horts.

So the decree was passed, and the crowds cheered, and then it was Wort Hort's turn. However, when the king gave him the same choice that he had given his uncle, Wort put his tongue in his cheek, grimaced horribly, and said he didn't know—he'd had so much fun being wicked.

"But thee have repented," the king reminded him.

A crafty light shone in Wort's eyes. "I only repented a little bit, mind you."

Now the king began to look so vexed that Silken turned and quickly whispered a few words to her mother, while good Gracious in turn repeated these to the king, who at once regained his gentle manner.

"Wort Hort," he said to the other, slowly and clearly, "instead of demoting thee to the kitchen scullery, where thee would do naught all day but sweep up bits of nutmeg shells and thus be known as Chore Hort"—here everybody shuddered—"we will grant to thee the office of Royal Choirmaster, in view of thy possessing a singularly beautiful singing voice

(which thee seldom permit anyone to hear). Thus
thee will entertain and delight all Horts at our fes-
tivities, from here on, and so be known as Choir Hort.
Will thee accept?"

Wort Hort, frowning, with his face squeezed up in
concentration as he tried to follow the king's long
speech, finally concluded that he should object and
was about to say as much, when Fat Hort (formerly
Uncle Rotten Hort) at his side muttered in his ear,
"Take it! Anything's better than Chore Hort, you
idiot!" So Wort nodded his head vigorously, looking
scared.

Unfortunately, the Royal Scribe, who was taking
all this down, was not very good at spelling, and
where he was supposed to write *Choir*, he wrote *Chore*
instead. Thus it went down in the Great Book of
Laws, and it could not be changed. This explains why
Wort Hort (known as Choir Hort, written as Chore
Hort) had to sweep nutmeg shells, anyway, but very
seldom, because he was so much in demand for his
singing. He was always called Choir Hort, too, as
we've said, even though everyone, including himself,
wrote it *Chore Hort*, not realizing the error.

So much for that. As soon as the decrees had been
read off and the Horts had cheered until they were
tired of the noise they were making, the king dis-
missed the officers. Then, turning to Cam, he was

about to address him, when he and everyone else saw that the boy was entirely encased in a thin coat of ice, behind which his anxious gaze stared at them in silent appeal.

"Forevermore!" cried Tee-Bo, and, running up to the boy in the greatest alarm, he threw himself at him, which caused Cam to topple over. The ice shattered and left him sitting on the cavern floor in a great puddle.

"Oh!" cried Silken in dismay. Rushing over to him, she removed the medallion from about her neck and placed it around his, looking deeply concerned.

"Th-th-thank you," Cam managed to say, rising and looking with chagrin at the water on the floor. "I tr-tried t-t-to s-say something, b-but m-my t-teeth st-stuck t-together!"

"Dear me," good Gracious now spoke up, "thee are all so chill, I fear some illness may come to thee, though thee have a wonderful pallor, to be sure!"

"It would be unwise," the king now declared, "for our friends to remain longer, though we would indeed desire to have thee reside here." (Cheers again from the Horts.) "We must part now," he continued, smiling his most winning smile, "but in a fortnight, thee must return to the country of the Horts to be the guests of honor at a wedding which is to take place at that time."

Silken hid her face in her curls, and Curly Hort straightened his shoulders and looked manlier than ever, while such resounding cheers rose on all sides that the rock walls trembled, and it was recorded as a minor earthquake at the university thirty miles away.

"Th-thank you," Cam said. Though he was slowly drying, he still kept swallowing pieces of melting ice.

"We accept your kind invitation very gladly," Carlyle said, in her mother's best manner.

Tee-Bo said, "Likewise," and then said, "Forevermore!" and looked embarrassed.

Cam returned Silken's medallion, and the three were escorted to the Great Door by the Guards of the Door, the Horts waving furiously and cheering mightily, and poor Cam stumbling because his feet were still numb with the cold.

Outside in the forest, the sun was sending its warm, golden light into the ferniest, darkest places, and there was a little warm wind rising and falling, sweet with the scent of pine and nutmeg.

"Wh-whew!" said Cam. "How wonderful the sun is!" He began an Indian war dance to get warm faster.

"I'm not cold now," Carlyle said, watching her brother. "Let's hurry home."

"You weren't soaked to the skin in the first place," Cam reminded her, and they had to wait five minutes while his clothes completely dried out and his teeth stopped chattering.

"Let's hurry!" Carlyle urged.

"The faster the better," Tee-Bo agreed.

"That's right; we're supposed to be home at four." Cam started running and jumping, catching at leaves and tossing sticks.

Tee-Bo ran along beside them. "I don't have to be home at four. I have another reason for hurrying."

"What?" asked the children.

"I have to look up that word in the dictionary," he said with an air of importance. "This is the first time I've ever been invited to a wedding—in a fortnight, too, whatever that means."

They all paused in the middle of the path.

"I don't know, either." Carlyle looked worried. "If it's at night, we'll never be allowed to go."

"Then they'll just have to change the time," Cam said, "because we're the guests of honor, and we have to be there."

They hurried homeward, and the minute they entered the house, they heard Mother talking on the phone.

"It was? . . . You did? . . . Really? . . . Well, forevermore! A goose! A *live* goose? . . . Yes, Idora, I most certainly will!"

When they came into the room, she was just putting the receiver back on the hook.

"Forevermore! Did you hear about Mrs. First-penny's goose?" were the first words she said to them.

"Her *goose?*" asked Cam.

"Her *goose!*" repeated Carlyle.

"Her *goose!*" exclaimed Tee-Bo, running up to her.

"It seems," Mother went on, some of Mrs. First-penny's excitement having transferred itself to her, "that what she discovered actually *was* an egg, and it hatched a goose!"

"A *goose!*" Cam said loudly.

"A *goose!*" screamed Carlyle.

"A *goose?*" snickered Tee-Bo, and he began running in circles around the room. "Well, forevermore!"

"But," added Mother, frowning somewhat, "how could the goose be full-grown, if it had just hatched?"

"Oops!" said Cam, but Mother went right on as if nothing had been said.

"I was going over to see her the minute I came home, but you are late, and Father wants me to make a Really Pie for dinner, so I guess—" Here she broke off, with a small exclamation. "Whatever have you children been doing? Cam, your clothes look as if you had worn them all summer, forevermore! And I suspect you haven't even had lunch! I should scold you, but you look like orphans, and I haven't the heart. Up, now! Into the tub! I want you all as fresh as daisies when Father gets home, and this time I want that shower turned off all the way!"

"Aren't we going to Mrs. Firstpenny's?" Carlyle asked as they turned to go upstairs.

"We'll go tomorrow. She has company now. While we were talking on the phone, someone drove up in a big truck."

"The poultry commissioner!" Cam murmured, struck once more with guilt.

"Yes," remarked Mother, whose hearing was sometimes uncomfortably acute, "that's what she said. She'd been waiting all afternoon for him. I wonder what *he* thought of the goose!"

"I hope he didn't say it out loud," Tee-Bo sighed as he followed the children upstairs. "Ethel's very sensitive about such things."

19
Fame Comes to Mrs. Firstpenny

The next day Mother tried to persuade Father to walk over to Mrs. Firstpenny's with her, but Father replied that he had never heard of anything so ridiculous in all his life as a full-grown goose hatching from an egg and said he preferred staying home to work on his Mongolian-English dictionary.

"On a day like this?" Mother would use any excuse, no matter how flimsy, to get out into the woods.

"My dear," Father replied kindly, "on any day of the year, the Mongol tongue, no matter how difficult, is simplicity itself compared with the vagaries of Mrs. Firstpenny's flights of imagination."

The children, having fully recovered from the emotional chaos of the day before, were on tenterhooks, waiting to get to Mrs. Firstpenny's. Mother was not in such a hurry. She liked to see the grass, bugs, rocks, shadows, and clouds. When they reached Farrow's Pond, the water was like a sheet of glass, unrippled from shore to shore.

"I must do an etching of this," Mother said, "before winter sets in. It has never been more beautiful."

"Oh, Mother," Carlyle called, skipping ahead, "do hurry! Mrs. Firstpenny is waiting!"

Tee-Bo bounded up beside her, casting a sympathetic glance at the little girl's worried face.

"Don't fret. I'm sure Ethel is very adjustable. Look how long she was at the poultry farm, which wasn't half as nice as being at Mrs. Firstpenny's."

"I worry about Mrs. Firstpenny, too," Carlyle sighed. "It was cruel to take the Great Wet-Stone away from her."

When they reached the edge of the woods, they could see the old lady sitting in the rocker on her porch.

"She's waiting for us," Mother said, waving.

Carlyle ran ahead, secretly wondering if they would find their friend in tears and what she would do if she were. But the sight that met her eyes made her stop short. Mrs. Firstpenny was rocking placidly, her knitting in her lap. On the porch swing opposite was a great mass of feathers, with a bright eye peering out.

"Isn't she beautiful?" The old lady sighed and looked tenderly at Ethel.

Carlyle stared anxiously to see if she was all right. "Oh, Ethel," she murmured, sinking down on the porch beside her, "I was so worried about you!"

"Well," breathed Mother, joining the others on the porch, "this most certainly is a goose!"

Ethel obligingly flapped down so Mother could take her seat on the swing.

"Carlyle called her Ethel just now," Mrs. Firstpenny said musingly. "I think it just suits her!"

"It ought to," Tee-Bo remarked. "It's her name."

"I've never known a goose named Ethel before," Mother answered politely, with a quick little look at her daughter. "What a large goose!" she said then. "Were you not at all startled to find her in your house, Idora?"

"You know"—the old lady stopped rocking and placed her knitting, which she had picked up to work on, back on her lap—"I think Ethel—yes, I am going to name her Ethel—I think she is going to be as much company to me as dear Mr. Firstpenny was. There he used to sit, on the porch swing, and when I'd look at him, he'd wake up and look at me with one eye, just as friendly and companionable as can be! Now, my dear, talk about startled—"

"Come around the back," Tee-Bo whispered to the children at this point. "Ethel wants to tell you something."

The children went around the house to the tire swing in back. Ethel waddled down the stairs after them.

"Ask her if Mrs. Firstpenny was afraid of her at first," Carlyle said hurriedly, bending over to stroke the quivering feathers, while Cam took the tire swing.

"Not a bit," the dog replied as the goose relayed the answer to him. "Ethel was very quiet and did just as she was told. When Mrs. Firstpenny walked in and saw her sitting in the center of the table where the Great Wet-Stone had been, she clapped her hands and cried, 'Oh, glory be! My egg's hatched!' This shook Ethel up a bit, but she got right over it. She says we were right about Mrs. Firstpenny. She's mad about her. Says she's ever so much better company than another goose."

Cam stood up, giving the swing to his sister.

"What about the poultry commissioner?"

"Hah!" Tee-Bo curled his upper lip as if in derision. "*That* chap fared all right! Mrs. Firstpenny had just made a fresh batch of custard and jelly doughnuts—they were still warm—and had carried the

ice-cream freezer in from the barn, full of fresh logan-
berry ice cream."

"Whew!" Cam whistled and raised his eyebrows.

"He ate seven doughnuts and had four cups of cof-
fee and two big bowlfuls of ice cream. Ethel said he
even patted her—after the third doughnut."

"But what did he say about . . . about . . . you
know—" Cam stopped, embarrassed.

"Hah!" the dog answered, exactly as before. "He
told her that anybody who could turn out ice cream
and doughnuts like that deserved to be rewarded. He
said she was lucky to have Ethel and vice versa. By
the way, Ethel is crazy about this place. She says
she—"

They were interrupted at this point by a loud
sound coming from the front of the house, like someone clicking his tongue against his teeth very fast.
Ethel's head jerked several times, and, with a hasty
look of apology to the others, she waddled off at top
speed.

"What was that?" asked Cam, and Tee-Bo trans-
lated quickly.

"That's Mrs. Firstpenny's special call for Ethel.
She usually has something nice for her to eat, but
Ethel says it will come in handy if the old lady ever
gets in trouble."

"Uncle Rotten Hort won't ever bother her again!"

Cam grinned and turned a cartwheel. "Ethel'd make mincemeat of him!"

"Impossible!" the dog sniffed with a superior air. "You can't make mincemeat of a Hort. It takes suet, raisins, apples. . . ."

The children, seeing the twinkle in his eyes, jumped up and grabbed him, had a quick tumble on the grass, and ran shrieking and laughing around the house to join the others on the porch.

20
Preparation for the Wedding

One day—it was a Saturday, exactly a fortnight after the Great Wet-Stone had been returned to the Horts —Mrs. Flanella happened to glance out her window at 36 Selah Road and see the McRae children, with their dog, headed up the street toward the bridge. She felt her forehead and then looked at the thermometer on the wall and nodded. It read eighty-three degrees.

"They must have colds," Mrs. Flanella decided and stared harder. Cam was wearing a stocking cap, earmuffs, and a stout winter jacket, plus mittens and boots. His sister had on a pretty blue and white ski

suit and carried a blanket over one arm. They were
as neat as two pins and appeared freshly scrubbed,
but Tee-Bo was the most dazzling of all. He had been
bathed and combed and brushed until every curl glis-
tened. A chrysanthemum was fastened above his
curly bangs, and he had been securely fitted into a
knit dog sweater of deep red with a white stripe at
the collar.

"I really should have had a carnation," he was saying as the trio hurried toward the bridge. "It's proper
for a gentleman to wear a carnation for an afternoon
wedding."

"We didn't have any." Carlyle glanced over her
shoulder. "Mrs. Flanella's watching. She thinks we're
crazy."

"Mother and Father will think so, too," Cam put
in grimly, "if they catch sight of us on their way back
from town! Hurry up!"

"How long can we stay?" panted the dog as they
increased their pace. "I'd hate to have to leave in the
middle."

"Mother's going to be sketching Farrow's Pond
late this afternoon," Carlyle told him. "We're supposed to meet her there."

They hurried on. In exactly forty minutes, the wedding of Silken and Curly would take place in the
great cavern.

As they passed Farrow's Pond, a hearty voice called out to them, and Matchlock's great head and shoulders appeared at the water's edge.

"Been waiting for you," he gurgled in his deep voice. "Have a bit of news."

"Don't detain us," Tee-Bo begged. "We have an important engagement." His whiskers trembled excitedly as he spoke.

"We're going to Curly and Silken's wedding," Carlyle explained.

The old fellow regarded them dubiously. "Pretty fancy duds, eh?"

"We'll freeze before it's over if we don't dress warmly," said Cam, whose face was as red as a beet. Even Tee-Bo, in his woolen sweater, was panting.

Matchlock nodded. "I'll be there. Going by the underground route. Keeps me from drying out, you know."

"I hope you'll sit with us during the ceremony," Carlyle said politely.

"Glad to, thank you," was the answer. "Now, do you want to hear my news? It's about your friend, the feathery one called Ethel."

"Get on with it, then, before we're late," urged Tee-Bo.

"The day she shot out of here," Matchlock began, with a wide and watery grin, "I didn't really get a good look at her. I suspect I was somewhat rude. All that cavorting in my pond, splashing about and so forth, made me forget my manners, by thunder."

"You weren't rude, Mr. Matchlock," Carlyle said. "You were upset."

"That's right, little girl," agreed the old fellow. "Glad to see you're so understanding. I thought you'd be pleased to hear that we've become friends, Ethel —that is, I and Ethel, heh-heh."

"You mean Ethel came back here?" asked Cam, surprised.

Matchlock nodded. "That girl is mad about my pond. Dotes on it. She was timid at first; just stood under the trees and stared. But I talked her out of that. Told her about my family and all, how distinguished we all are, and some of the history of the pond. It wasn't long before she realized how handsome—I mean, how friendly—we toads are. Heh-heh. Now she comes here every morning. Good company, too, by thunder!"

"Every morning?" asked Carlyle. "Does she stay long?"

"About an hour. Then back she goes to her mistress, straight as an arrow, in case she's needed. Great company, Ethel. Proud to know her."

Carlyle sighed and wrinkled her nose, from which a drop of perspiration was about to fall. "I wonder why we can't understand Ethel's language. We can talk to you, Mr. Matchlock."

"Oh, *that*." Matchlock ducked beneath the water and came up with bubbles winking all over him. "You know, Ethel's got a speech impediment. Real hard to understand, at first. It's sort of cute, I say. Told her so."

"That's splendid news," Tee-Bo remarked hastily, "but we'd better be getting on."

"See you at the wedding!" Carlyle said as they prepared to leave.

"Wait a minute!" called their friend. "You don't have another—ah, what do you call them? A dark and shivery one. Do you?"

"You mean an incantation?"

"Oh, that delicious word!" cried the giant toad, water droplets flying from him as he trembled. "It makes my blood run cold! Do you have one? A good, scary one? Do you?"

"Wedding days aren't incantation days," Cam declared firmly.

"You wouldn't want to go all shivery to a wedding," added Tee-Bo.

Matchlock looked crestfallen. "I wouldn't?"

"Don't worry, Mr. Matchlock," called Carlyle as they hurried off, "I know lots of shivery ones, and you shall hear them all!"

They could hear him gurgling with pleasure as they hastened toward the falls.

The wedding of Silken and Curly Hort was probably one of the most beautiful of all time. Though the children were to see several weddings during their years of growing up, the memory of this one would be cherished for the rest of their lives.

The great cavern was so brilliantly lighted that they could see nothing for a moment, after stepping out of the dark passageway. As far as the eye could reach, there were torches—in niches, hanging on walls, and standing on carved poles. Long streamers of entwined water lilies, of such waxen hue they looked unreal and exuding a heady fragrance, floated from the ceiling almost to the heads of the guests, while satin couches and long, glittering tables were spread throughout. Added to all this were fireflies, diaphanous creatures winging in circular flight overhead to shed even more light, in an array of colors that dazzled the eye. The Hort musicians, Kluge, Brock, and Camel, dressed in their finest, were playing a lively tune, and it seemed that the streamers of flowers, as well as the fireflies, were keeping time to the cadence.

Tee-Bo was shaking with excitement. "Forevermore, it's very formal, isn't it? I should have worn a dress suit! I hope no one is offended."

"We can't help how we're dressed," Cam muttered. "We'd freeze if we'd worn anything else!"

They were beginning to wish they hadn't bundled up so much, even though the great cavern was cool and filled with floating mists, as usual. They stood there, feeling quite out of place and miserable in the midst of the graceful and richly clad Hort merrymakers.

Suddenly a trumpet sounded, piercingly loud, and the music halted. The crowds on the floor instantly drew back, like waves of the sea, and opened a pathway for the newcomers, straight to the Royal Table. King Courtly and his family and officers had risen and were staring in the direction of their young guests. Pages in silver tunics stepped forward and politely took the children by the arm, leading them, amidst great cheers, right up to the royal family.

"Welcome, O noble benefactors, good Cameron, good Carlyle, and good Tee-Bo!" pronounced the king in solemn tones. At this the Horts let out a cheer that blew the fireflies dizzily about for a long moment, and the musicians went back to their instruments with a resounding crash of cymbals.

As soon as the cheering had died away, King Courtly requested that they be seated in their places of honor beside him and his queen, and then he in-

troduced them all around the table. Matchlock was
there, too, in an enormous chair provided just for
him. His manners were perfect, of course, as he sat
there, nodding pleasantly at everyone, except that he
could not resist uncurling his tongue at the fireflies
passing overhead and smacking his lips in contemplation of such delicate morsels, though he was not
impolite enough to actually nibble one. There were
fern cakes by the thousands, trillium tea in four different flavors, and a nutmeg cake seventeen layers
tall, frosted with what looked like pink bubbles.

"The wedding cake is made from the last of our
nutmeg," Courtly told them. "We have been hoard-
ing it, but now that is no longer necessary, since tomorrow we go to the Great Wood to harvest our nutmeg crop, thanks to you, our true friends."

The children could not say a word, because there
was so much clapping by the Horts. When things
were quieter, good Gracious said to the children, "We
are happy thee dressed warmly. It would grieve us
if thee were to suffer a chill and not stay for the
ceremony."

"The beast is well clad, also," King Courtly added,
smiling his approval at Tee-Bo.

"King Courtly," Cam said, when they were taking
their second cup of tea, "what makes the Great Wet-
Stone balance—" but he was cut short by a signal

from an unseen courtier to the king, who hastily put down his cup and rose from the table.

"Oh, my, the ceremony is about to begin!" Carlyle cried.

21
The Rock in Farrow's Pond

A great hush fell over the cavern of the Horts as the wedding of Silken and Curly commenced. Sweet strains of music began a hauntingly lovely song that the children had never heard before. From an entrance across the vast chamber, bearers entered, carrying between them a palanquin, or pillowed seat, and on this reposed a small figure, gorgeously clad. He was carried to the center of the cavern, where the palanquin was lowered, permitting him to step out and mount a raised platform nearby.

Turning first to the king and then to the musicians, he stood as tall as possible, for he was quite short, and then he began to sing.

"It's Wort Hort!" Carlyle gasped aloud as a beautiful voice sang out clearly and sweetly.

"Choir Hort," Gracious corrected kindly.

The former Wort Hort, now known as Choir Hort, indeed possessed a singing voice as unlike his former personality as is night from day. Now he sang a tender wedding song, of hope and of love and of the good years to come.

At the conclusion, there came another deep hush. The curtains parted to allow the young couple to make their entrance, Curly on one side with his retinue of young attendants and Silken on the other with hers, treading slowly across the wide floor to meet at a place just short of the Royal Table.

King Courtly stepped down, his queen following, and there, so close that the children and Tee-Bo could see and hear everything perfectly, he performed the ceremony himself, as befits a king.

As soon as the ceremony was over and the wedding march had been played five times and everyone had shaken hands with the handsome couple, Cam saw his chance to speak to the king.

"King Courtly," said he, "how does the Great Wet-Stone balance itself?"

His old friend gazed at him thoughtfully for a moment before replying. "It is a good question, and thee

are a bright lad. I wish I could say I know the answer, but such is not strictly true."

"We have all asked this question," Curly Hort said, approaching from the dance floor with his bride on his arm, "for it has confounded our scholars and mystics. But the king will tell thee somewhat more of our mysterious Stone."

"Long ago," King Courtly began, nodding pleasantly at his new son-in-law, "sometime between the fifteenth and eighth centuries B.C. of your time reckoning, the planet Earth was visited by a fiery comet that caused great damage and precipitated many changes in the country of the Horts. Our underground rivers spouted geysers as high as mountains, our tranquil inner seas raged, and we were in danger of becoming gravely overheated from the flow of hidden volcanic lava. One day this strangely beautiful stone —which we call our Great Wet-Stone—rolled up onto the shore of one of our oceans and was found by the great Pan Hort himself."

As the good king spoke, the music quieted down, and as many as could drew near to hear this tale from the lips of their beloved monarch, for it was a true history and one that they never tired of hearing. Good Gracious silently filled her husband's cup with more trillium tea and then settled back to listen as he continued.

"Instantly, all turmoil ceased. The seas were tranquil, and the earth was quiet. As soon as the mystical properties of the Stone were discovered, the Horts put them to good use, for from that day on, they were able, by carrying with them one of the smaller stones concealed in the Great Wet-Stone, to go to the Great Wood to harvest the nutmeg, without danger of broiling or turning to leather from the heat of your sun.

"Some say," the king went on reflectively, "that the touch of Pan Hort himself gave the Stone the power to balance, but our scientists have a different explanation. They believe that it is composed partly of matter from Earth and partly of matter fallen from the great comet, and so, obeying two different sets of physical laws, it is in constant opposition to itself. Thus, in a state of eternal siege, so to speak, it cannot move either way and so remains stationary. Is this clear to thee, lad?"

"No," said Cameron gravely, "it is not."

The king sighed. "Nor to anyone else, I must confess. But it is all we know."

"Ask Father," Tee-Bo said. "He might know."

The king would have talked more, but the Horts were eager now to dance, which they loved second only to singing, so the signal was given, and the music began. The children and the dog remained seated, watching the dazzling display of colored lights and the twirling figures of the dancers, while Matchlock, who had had somewhat more than his fill of nutmeg cake and trillium tea, threatened to fall asleep and tumble from his chair.

"Ho-ho-ho," the toad yawned when Carlyle tugged at him to waken him. "Not napping, not at all. Just closed my eyes a bit." But when this happened three more times, the old fellow decided he had had enough.

"Say my good-byes to the king and queen," he requested, "and I'll just slip away, back to my pond. Ethel may drop over, and I'd like to be there if she does. Don't forget to stop by, now!" Then, with a thump-thump, the old toad made his way to the underground river a little distance off and vanished, with a million bubbles, in its depths.

Presently the children began feeling cold, in spite of their heavy garments, and after Tee-Bo sneezed three times, Cam decided they should take their leave. "Before we turn to ice and spoil everything," he explained.

King Courtly and good Gracious bade them a fond farewell, while Silken took their hands and made them promise to return soon. Curly Hort was so proud of his bride that all he could do was stare and sigh, but he did remember his manners and said, on parting, "Thee have saved all our lives. Call on us whenever thee may need us."

"Also," added the king, "whenever thee are nearby and hear the voice of the Hort, know that we are in the Great Wood harvesting nutmeg and come join us, for this is a time of much festivity among our people."

The children and Tee-Bo promised, and at last all good-byes were said. They were cheered again and escorted to the passageway, where the Horts stopped, because they went into the Great Wood only to harvest the crop and never at any other time.

Once the children were outside the falls, they began running and throwing themselves about in the sunshine, until their hair was wild and their clothes were full of stickers and leaves.

"Wasn't it a beautiful wedding!" shouted Cam, doing several cartwheels.

"Yes, but this sunshine is best of all!" Carlyle shrieked, tumbling about on the ground with Tee-Bo.

For over two hours, they had been so still in the misty chill of the cavern that now it was sheer joy to run and shout and feel the hot sun pouring over them.

"Of one thing I'm sure," declared Cam, pulling off his stocking cap and mittens. "I'm glad I'm not a Hort."

"But they're almost the nicest people in the whole world," his sister said as a drop of melted ice rolled off one eyebrow and down her cheek.

"Except for Uncle Rotten Hort," Cam replied.

"Which reminds me," Tee-Bo exclaimed, "that we didn't see him at all! Where was he?"

"In the Royal Kitchen," replied Carlyle. "Good Gracious told me he likes his new job so much that he stays there all the time, thinking up new recipes."

"Let's go back," said Tee-Bo, licking his lips hungrily, "in a fortnight—which isn't a night at all but means two weeks! I looked that up myself in the dictionary," he added proudly.

Cam shrugged. "I just asked Father. It was quicker that way."

"And I asked Mother," put in Carlyle. Then she placed one hand quickly over her mouth, her eyes widening. "Mother's waiting at Farrow's Pond for us!"

At this the three ran off through the wood and soon arrived at the pond lying dappled with shadows and sunlight.

"Mother!" cried Carlyle as they ran up to her. "Have you been here long?"

Mother was seated on the grassy slope, sketching the scene before her, but when the children came into view, her pencil paused in midair.

"Whatever—" she began, staring in disbelief at their clothing. "Oh, forevermore!" Tee-Bo came up to see the sketch, and she reached down to remove the red sweater with the white stripe. "Poor boy," she murmured, rumpling his fur affectionately. "Does that feel better?"

"Yes, it does," he said, nodding. "Thank you."

"My children," Mother went on, "it is eighty in the shade. It is *not* snowing, unless I am suffering delusions."

Cam shook his head while he and Carlyle pulled off their heavy attire.

"You're right. We're roasting."

"Then, how do you explain these clothes?"

"Oh," her son replied, with a quick look at the other two, "we've been having an adventure, you see."

"And it's over?" Mother questioned hopefully.

"All over."

"Then," she said with a sigh of relief, "you'll find lunch in the basket here. It's just ordinary food"—for a moment mother looked almost wistful—"not magic or anything. . . ."

Carlyle dived into the bag. "Like ordinary peanut butter and mustard sandwiches!" she shrieked in delight and began munching and rolling her eyes in rapture. As she did so, she caught sight of the sketch. It was a drawing of Farrow's Pond, from where they stood, done delicately but firmly, so that everything was there: the sweep of the willow branches that trailed across the surface, the pebbly shore, the rise of the hill in the background.

"What's that?" asked Carlyle, pointing carefully at the sketch without touching it. Down in one corner was a mammoth stone set in a strange position, almost as though crouching.

Mother looked at it thoughtfully while Cam and Tee-Bo came up to look. "You know," she said after a moment, "when I drew that rock—or whatever it was—it was really there." She nodded at them, then stared across the pond. "But now it's gone. I took my eyes off it for only a moment to watch a big white bird flying over, and when I looked again, it was gone."

The children and the dog exchanged glances, their eyes dancing. Mother bent closer to examine the rock she had sketched.

"Forevermore," she exclaimed softly, "it looks just like a giant toad!"